J.C. COSTA

The Demon's Trial

TRAFFORD
PUBLISHING™

Note for Librarians: A cataloguing record for this book is available from Library and Archives
Canada at www.collectionscanada.ca/amicus/index-e.html
ISBN 1-4120-8636-1

Printed in Victoria, BC, Canada. Printed on paper with minimum 30% recycled fibre.
Trafford's print shop runs on "green energy" from solar, wind and other environmentally-friendly power sources.

TRAFFORD
PUBLISHING™
Offices in Canada, USA, Ireland and UK

Book sales for North America and international:
Trafford Publishing, 6E–2333 Government St.,
Victoria, BC V8T 4P4 CANADA
phone 250 383 6864 (toll-free 1 888 232 4444)
fax 250 383 6804; email to orders@trafford.com
Book sales in Europe:
Trafford Publishing (UK) Limited, 9 Park End Street, 2nd Floor
Oxford, UK OX1 1HH UNITED KINGDOM
phone 44 (0)1865 722 113 (local rate 0845 230 9601)
facsimile 44 (0)1865 722 868; info.uk@trafford.com
Order online at:
trafford.com/06-0392

10 9 8 7 6 5 4 3 2

Prologue

I was still dizzy when I sat down to watch another videotape. A child was climbing into the lion's enclosure. I watched the tape and, gradually, as I saw his two legs already on the other side of the fence, I began to faint. Luckily, before I totally lost consciousness, I had enough time to warn some colleagues who were working nearby about my imminent collapse.

It only lasted a couple of minutes, but during that time I dreamt something important, something essential; the trouble is, I do not remember what.

A few minutes later I found myself on the floor surrounded by people trying to wake me up. It was not long before the paramedics began asking me questions and checking me out. I was confused at first, but later I remembered the accident with clarity.

That afternoon I had been watching some videotapes of one of my zoo inspections when I realised I was unsure which zoo I was viewing—too many visits in a relatively short period of time. I was in a hurry because a TV producer was waiting for a compilation tape. I had to put together the relevant shots, and then write a list with the names of the zoos and the animals in them.

I was almost done; I just had one zoo I could not remember. I had to rush, so I thought that if I went downstairs—to my office—I could then check on the computer which zoos had Asiatic lions, and perhaps I would remember. I did go downstairs, and I did it very fast; too fast in fact, because I tripped on my way down. I was going to fall flat on my chest—and probably break some important bones in my body—but luckily I had the reflexes to hold on to the handrail and pull up. I was hoping that I would have enough space to move my legs forward so I could land on my feet (the 'wasp manoeuvre', I later called it). It worked, but it worked too well; I did land on my feet, but only after crashing my head against the wooden beam on the ceiling.

I did not lose consciousness then; I was in a lot of pain, but I did not pass out. Interestingly, though, I suddenly remembered the name of the zoo I had forgotten. I might have had it on the tip of my tongue and the impact made me spit it out. Rubbing my head I walked around the office reassuring everybody that the noise they had heard was nothing more serious than my unfortunate, but relatively harmless, pirouette. Still in pain I went back upstairs to watch the tape again and confirm that my sudden improvement in memory was reliable. I sat down and, well, you know the rest.

I explained the story to the paramedics, so after a few checks they advised me to go to the hospital—for some x–rays—just to be sure. Once there the doctors performed many tests and concluded that everything was fine; that appeared to be the end of the adventure. In fact, though, it was quite the opposite; that was the beginning. It was the beginning because from that moment on I realised I was pregnant; it was now obvious to me; I was pregnant with a book.

I know, you are now confused. You are not sure whether I am a man or a woman; you are not sure what I do for living; you are not even sure of my nationality or the country in which I am writing this. At this stage you should already know, but you see, this is my first book. I haven't much experience of writing; it does not come naturally to me. So, let me help you a little bit.

I am—what is normally known as—a man; 37 years old, not very tall, not very thin and, as you may have already guessed, English is not my mother language—you would have noticed if you had heard my accent, anyway. I consider myself a scientist, but I now work inspecting zoos for a British animal welfare organisation. I am what we call a Zoo Checker (a new term we use to describe an investigator specialised in captive animals). This is what I do, and this is what I was doing when I realised I had a book inside me. It was there, kicking, and it seemed as if it were due soon.

Since my head accident I'd had an unstoppable urge to write a book. Perhaps it was something to do with the dream I had had while I was unconscious—I still cannot remember it. Perhaps it was something to do with my memory, and the realisation that it can be lost as quickly as it can be found. Perhaps it was my workaholism, and my 'stressful' life that made me carelessly run everywhere. Perhaps it was my age, and the way my body began

3

telling me about it. I do not know, but I was sure that a book was coming, and it was coming soon.

I hadn't a clue what the book was supposed to be about. Was it a fiction book, a scientific book, a biography? I did not know, but the important thing was to find a place to deliver it. It had to be a place where it could come out undisturbed; a sheltered place, sheltered from this world; a place where people do not go, where people do not stay; somewhere remote and isolated, somewhere quiet; somewhere up North.

PART ONE

Chapter One
December 10th 2001

I got to the train on time, as I always do, but it got delayed, as it often does. This meant that the trip was going to be slightly longer than expected, which did not bother me much, to be honest. The longer the trip, the better my acclimatisation process would be. From Brighton to the Scottish Highlands; this is almost as far as you can go in Great Britain without toppling into the sea.

During the first hours we travelled through dense fog — honestly, this is not a cheap literary description. It was as if the landscape had been banned for a while — or perhaps it was a sign that I had to write a London–detective–type book, who knows? I was still looking for a subject to write about, and I was hoping it would come if I paid enough attention to the world around me. With nothing to see outside and nothing interesting inside, my mind began wandering.

I have noticed, for quite a long time now, a distinctive quality in travelling North/South as opposed to East/West. The latter is a trip through humanity, where culture is the changing landscape. The former, on the other hand, is a trip through Earth, where Nature is the changing landscape. It is almost a change in planet; different daylight, different climate, different vegetation, different stars, and even a different gravitational pull. The people also change, but they change because the planet changes under them.

I wonder whether this fundamental difference in geographical migration rooted human evolution from the start. Early people, the first humans under our genus *Homo*, moved north from central or southern Africa finding a new planet, and becoming new species along the way. When they travelled east, though, their species did not change — this is one theory, anyway.

I wonder whether the motivation behind my trip to Scotland has some parallels with the motivation of those first migrating humans who attempted cross–latitudinal travel. Were they escaping from something? Were they looking for something they did not have? Were they aimlessly wandering north without even noticing it? Was I escaping? Was I looking for something new, or being dragged north by a supernatural power? The truth is that I was going north because it was the only place I could imagine myself in isolation long enough so I could write my book undisturbed. Perhaps the first *Homo* also looked for a place with fewer people. They were prepared to face cold and darkness in order to have a little peace away from other human creatures — also known as human beings. Well, it seems we haven't made much progress in all these years, have we?

I was glad I was travelling by train, rather than by

plane. I did not want to fall onto the North planet unprepared. After all, we are in December, and the Highland winter can be quite harsh. I would rather land on it softly, allowing myself to witness the subtle changes in landscape, temperature and light. Besides, train was cheaper, which helped.

Why did I have to write the book in 23 days? Convenience, really. I did not want to take too much time off, so I would not miss the plot of all the campaigns and investigations I was involved in—I am a workaholic, remember? Also, it seemed somehow possible to write a book in 23 days; at least the first draft. This was as much as I aspired to for this trip; the first draft. I knew it was mad, but I really could not take more time off. Moreover, I am known for doing things fast. I speak fast, I eat fast and I walk fast; I should be able to write a book fast too—it does not need to be *War and Peace*, does it?

By going to Scotland in winter, and by being disconnected from the rest of the world, it was as if I was putting myself at the edge of a pool table pocket. No matter how bad I was at pool, all the odds would be in favour of me potting the ball. I would have no choice other than be to be inspired and to write. There are plenty of possibilities in this quantum world, but the highest probability was pointing towards the same conclusion; the birth of a book.

Before we got to Newcastle the fog disappeared. Due to the fact that the sun was shining right into my face I could see how high in latitude we already were (i.e. it was about one in the afternoon and the sun was quite low on the horizon). If I had been in the tropics the sun would

9

have been high in the sky, but up there it forced me to close my eyes for most of the trip. I was sitting facing south, you see, in order to see where I was coming from; but with the sun on my face I could not see anything, so I looked into my dreams instead.

I am that sort of person that dreams anywhere, even when I am still totally awake—more often if I am in motion, as in a car, in a train or even walking. Because I had to close my eyes all the time it is not a surprise that I started daydreaming on the train to Scotland.

I remembered the first time I went to the Highlands. It was my second year in England, still unable to speak English properly. I had left Barcelona with one backpack on the front and another on the back, and I had tried, unsuccessfully, to settle down in several other countries before attempting the UK. I was looking for a place where I could continue my career as a zoologist, and at the same time develop my interests in animal conservation and welfare. I found that it was very difficult to achieve this goal in Barcelona, despite the fact that the Catalan culture (Barcelona is the capital of Catalonia, by the way) seemed more animal friendly than the Spanish one. Britain had always been in the back of my mind as the place where such goals could be achieved, so when I arrived to this country with my two bags I knew straight away that I had found a new home.

Needless to say, though, that before trying to continue with my work I had to learn the language, I had to find a place to live, a job and all that. I decided to spend my winters in London doing any sort of work—to survive—and to hitch hike around the rest of the UK during the summer to see whether I could find a place where I could be an Animal Welfare Zoologist. This is how I got to the Highlands the first time.

I was fascinated by the landscape. I hadn't much experience of cold climate ecosystems, so everything was new to me. I walked miles and miles without seeing anyone. Sleeping in my tent, getting a lift from the occasional car, seeing my first seals and otters, getting stuck in the pits and being eaten by the midges—all terribly exciting. Those days—almost a decade away now—always ended with an intense feeling of achievement; nothing to lose, and everything to win.

And here I was going to the Highlands again, although this time with many things to lose—a job, a flat, and many possessions—a bit older, and by train. We had been travelling for hours and the landscape had not changed much. Alien graffiti, leafless trees, red–bricked houses, sheep–spotted fields, linked metal giants and fully populated spaces. Whether or not it was cold outside, all my senses were oblivious to it.

I had left most of England behind, and soon I was going to beat my fellow Mediterranean cousins—the Romans—in their first attempt to make this journey. A wee while later I saw some tartan on other passengers in my coach, and I heard some rolled 'r's popping out every now and then in people's conversations. They were probably there before, but I did not notice them. Is this what nations are really about, being noticed? How many wars have been fought for not having paid enough attention?

Eventually, things began changing outside. I could see

now fewer populated spaces, more sheep–spotted fields, and fewer red bricks; we were getting somewhere. The sun was still on my face, but it seemed somehow further away; in fact, it was further away, just a little bit.

We got to Edinburgh and I had to change train. Soon after, when the sun was already well below the horizon and fog was coming out of everybody' s mouths, I was impatiently looking at my watch and waiting for the departure of my train to Stirling. Frost covered the track, and salt was seasoning the platforms. It already seemed another planet, different from Brighton anyway.

This time I was sitting facing north—I did not seem to care any more about Romans, Anglo–Saxons or Mods. The more I continued travelling, the more ice seemed to have conquered more land; I thought that tennis courts were a particularly symbolic conquest—this planet had a sense of humour.

I had to wait for a short while in Stirling station. After a couple of minutes waiting I took my scarf from my pocket and I wrapped it around my neck. A couple of minutes later I took the gloves out of my pocket and put them on. A couple of minutes more and I thought of taking out my woolly hat, but I resisted the temptation; I only had to wait a few more minutes to take the train to Inverness. By then, it was completely dark, and a cup of tea and a cheese sandwich were on the cards.

Three hours to Inverness did not show me much of the outside world; pitch black outside, bright fluorescent light inside. If you looked at the windows you could only see an infinite reflection of yourself—my parietal baldness had been endlessly multiplied. Perhaps this is what it was going to be like from now on; unable to see the world as I know it, I would be lost in an endless reflection of myself—the only thing bothering me being my premature baldness. I was going too fast, I was getting too excited, and I was drunk on symbolism. I realised that the best thing I could do was to close my eyes and doze off.

I dreamt that I was zoo checking in Somerset—don't ask me why—and that I had been spotted by the staff of the zoo I was investigating. We normally work *in cognito*, otherwise we could be asked to leave, or instead any possible malpractice or problem could then be miraculously swept away from our view. Most of the time zoo staff do not even realise we are there filming—this is for people such as me, full–time professional Zoo Checkers—but in my dream they did spot me, and they chased me all over the place with burning torches and sharp forks. I have had this sort of dream before, but they always end well. I normally manage to escape unharmed with all the evidence I needed for the case I was working on. This time was not an exception; I was awoken by the sound of the train doors opening, before the angry mob of zoo directors even got close to me.

Every now and then we stopped in a station—this was a slow train. Only in those stops did I get a short glimpse of the outside world; not much, usually just the name of the station. But now the names were in pairs, in English and Gaelic. It was as if, up there, there were not enough people who cared to delete one of them. Perhaps there were not enough people who cared to learn English at all. This was a good sign; I was heading in the right direction.

Inverness was as far north as I would go. In fact, it is almost as far north as anyone can go by train in Britain. I finally added my woolly hat to my clothing setting myself the task of finding a B&B, spending the night there, and resuming my trip in the morning. It had already been thirteen hours since I left Brighton, and I could not travel any more that day.

The B&B I found was quite nice — with my job, I have slept in many of them, so I am qualified to judge. An electric blanket already switched on was trying to tell me something. I turned the TV set on to watch it for the last time before I would self–impose a regime of broadcasting deprivation. A documentary about an Italian arctic explorer gave an ironic touch to the evening — he was rescued after his dirigible crashed, in case you were wondering.

The electric blanket gave me very sweet dreams indeed, and the first day of my journey ended well.

Chapter Two
December 11th 2001

Next day I was back on the road before sunrise — not that I was particularly early; the sun was particularly late. I had my full anti–cold gear on, and it worked. The sun was already rising when my train to Strathcarron left the station. This time it was not a trip to another planet, as on the day before — I was already on that new planet. Now it was time to travel through cultures; leave the Scottish, move through the Celts, and hopefully get as close as I can to virgin territory. Now it was time to go west.

I was on my own in the train — nobody wanted to go where I was going, another good sign. There were no clouds around, and another sunny day was waiting for me. Frost was still noticeable on the grey roofs, and sea gulls had already signed on for the day. You could still see the moon, in its waning phase, pointing toward the East where the oranges were beating the purples. Minutes after we left the station we were travelling parallel to water; would Nessy be up at this time? Probably not; not because it is too early, but because it is too late—a few million years late, in fact.

The leafless trees looked purple to me; maybe a combination of frost, early morning light, and the train speed. In fact, everything looked purplish—this was indeed another planet. I could already see snow on the purple glens, and ice and frost everywhere else. Sheep were not so conspicuous anymore—the fields did not seem infected with them as before. We turned slightly to the right, so for a short while I could see how the battle of colours was doing; oranges, now helped by yellows, were still ahead.

Eventually, the sun stopped the colours game and decided to join us for the day, and the frost, as if it had been brought from Romania, vanished away. We stopped under a bridge where I could read: "Don't let the Johns get you down"—even up here graffiti has found room for political expression. We were not west enough yet, too much civilisation. The driver pushed the button, got back on the train, and we all resumed our journey.

At one point we seemed to abandon humanity drastically; we were going through the wilderness. The frost there was not Romanian anymore; many trees had leaves—the Scottish pines seemed to know that this is what we call them. A loch on the right perfectly reflected the already sunny glens, with not a ripple to distort the image. A few miles ahead I noticed somebody on a hill close to the track. We were watched by a local, and after a couple of seconds she ran away; a few others followed her some metres along the line—I suppose deer have got the right to distrust us, even when we are on a train.

I wanted to ignore the RAF jet that flew above the train and disappeared between the valleys, but I could not. I noticed the fences, the road, and the telephone poles — we were not west enough yet.

We finally arrived at my station; from there, the rest of the trip was going to be by car. A work mate that lives in the Highlands had kindly offered to drive me to my final destination, where no trains or buses can go. It was so far west that it was beyond Great Britain itself. It was on an island; the Isle of Skye.

Once on the island we stopped at a supermarket, and there I bought all the consumables I would need for my 23 day stay. Without a car I would be unable to go to a shop and buy anything; the cottage, which had been generously offered to me by a friend of a friend, was miles away from the nearest shop. I had to buy everything, and I did; the question is, did I buy enough? Only time will tell.

After shopping we continued into the deepest and most isolated end of the island. We had to look for a ruined castle on the shore, and the cottage should be close by. Being the only visible car for miles, we followed the one–track road and we finally spotted the castle. I had some instructions about how to get to the cottage that had been sent to me by the owners — whom I had not met — together with the keys. In the letter there was information about how to turn the electricity on, when to take the rubbish bag out and all that, but not a detailed description of the cottage; they just said that it had a corrugated iron roof. We saw one that could be it — although it did not correspond to what we thought was the right house number. I stepped out of the car and walked up the muddy path up to the gate. Once there I shouted, but the cottage seemed deserted. It did have the right roof—now that I could see it up close—but somehow it seemed too big for what I had imagined. I went around it, getting repeatedly stuck in the mud, and eventually I decided to open the gate and have a closer look. There was only one way to be sure; to try the key. I did, which confirmed to me that the cottage was going to be my home for the next 23 days.

The house was much better than I had expected. It certainly had more 'stuff', and it was bigger than I had thought it would be. It had four bedrooms, and they all looked charmingly rustic and cosy. Its isolation was perfect, and the view stunning. Trees at the back, sea at the front, hills on the left, and an abandoned castle on the right—with some impressive mountains behind it. I wanted it for life.

It did not take long before I had my first mini adventure. I had taken all the bags and food into the cottage, so my friend was free to leave me there. But her car did not seem to agree; it decided instead to dig a big hole in the ground, as if it was planning to bury a bone. We did the usual in these cases; dig beneath the wheel, put a plank under, push, panic, etc. Of all the plans, looking for local help proved to be the most effective. Eventually, help arrived, so my friend could at last leave me there. Very excited at having been abandoned in such a beautiful and isolated spot, I said goodbye completely covered in mud. This was going to be fun.

It took me some time to operate the house properly. I could not manage to turn on the water until a monkey wrench did the job, the gas bottles seemed to be filled with non–combustible gas, hot water was suffering an identity crisis, and little things like that. Before I realised it, the sun hid itself away—I thought it was very early because it really was very early, before four. For some reason I believed that it was imperative I put everything in place before dark; the food on the shelves, the clothes in the drawers, the books on the table, the sleeping bag on the bed, etc—as if I would not be able to do it at night. I rushed and I managed to do it on time; I was still trapped in a world of deadlines.

When everything seemed in order I made a cup of tea, a sardine sandwich, and I sat down. Then, for the first time, I heard it, loud and clear, as I had not heard it for years. Almighty, unmistakable, definite; a deep, absolute silence. The absence of any form of noise whatsoever was so conspicuous, so noticeable, that one could not do anything other than listen. As an air vacuum sucks up everything in reach, a complete silence attracts total attention. That might well be the sound that was going to be with me most of my time at the cottage, but right then I was hearing it totally unaccustomed, so I could not ignore it. The silence was so perfect that after a short while I could even hear my blood rushing through my ears; I could hear my own pulse. No wind, no insects, no birds, no waves, just my body keeping me alive. I sat there for ages, not capable of moving, mesmerised by the unexpected voice of my heart. The perception of my own reaction fed back the magic of the moment. Silence, loneliness, emptiness, death... The fridge turning itself on broke the silence and freed me from my trance.

Through the window I saw the remnants of what was probably a spectacular sunset, but I did not want to go out and watch it. The silence had scared me a little bit, and a beautiful sunset can sometimes hurt — too much at once, I thought. Everything in its time; there was going to be one of those every day. I stood up, and I brushed away all transcendence off my clothes.

Once dark, the temperature dropped considerably. Moving up and down, and after the car incident, I had been keeping myself warm — in fact, I thought that the cottage was not cold, considering. After dark, though, I felt the Highlands. I plugged several of the electrical heaters in, and I lit a fire — luckily, I had all that was required for the task. The fire went quite well, but it did not last very long. — I am sure that by the end of my stay I will be proficient in eternal fires. For now, it was OK, but the cottage did not seem to have warmed enough; condensation could occasionally still be seen coming out of my mouth. Definitively the Highland darkness was going to be my main behavioural enrichment.

It was time to test the waters and see how the cold would affect my work. I took the backpack, I pulled a plastic bag and from it and I took my laptop computer out. I decided to put it on the oak kitchen table; it seemed the most appropriate place to work, with the food and the fire. An old rusty electric fire on the left, an almost extinguished real fire on the right, a lovely oak piece of furniture with china plates and bizarre containers in front of me, and a window with a blue tartan curtain behind me. All ready, I pushed the 'start' button.

The laptop sounded like a hurricane; the small fan in

the processor had the chance to blow free of any other oppressing sound. Millions of other mechanical noises joined in, as if within the flat and stylish computer body there were thousands of old fashioned clocks ticking. I am still unsure about the origin of all those noises, but the computer seemed to need them to operate comfortably, so I let them be.

And here I am now, typing away. It feels cold, the fire is out, it is only half past seven but it seems midnight, and I am not quite sure about what is going to happen. But one thing I am certain of; coming here to write a book was a good idea.

Chapter Three
December 12th 2001

The first night at the cottage was quite interesting. I discovered — to my pleasure — that the bed I had chosen to sleep in had a functioning electric blanket — I suppose that up here such blankets are as much of a given as a fan is in a Brazilian hotel. It worked quite well, but it created a huge difference in temperature between the parts of my sleeping bag that touched the blanket, and the parts that did not. Every time I moved and my body touched any of the non–heated parts I woke up as if water had been poured on me. In the morning all the exterior of my sleeping bag was wet, so I had to hang it to dry — I will need to perfect my sleeping procedures.

At about eight in the morning the sun was already reaching Skye, so it seemed a good time to get up. Once the sun was shining away I checked the small thermometer I had left outside; it had just reached zero degrees Celsius — another beautiful day without clouds, possibly not too cold. The best I could do was to spend the daylight hours exploring the area, and to see how long would it take me to get to the next village, just in case I needed to go.

I went downstairs and the kitchen smelled of lovely burnt wood. Porridge seemed a good breakfast option. I decided I would wait until the frost had gone, and then I would pick up my cameras and go exploring. The day before I had written about my trip to the cottage; I had hoped that by writing what was happening to me, the book in my head would be encouraged to come out. I did not want to force things; writing about what I see, feel and think would hopefully make me write about who I am, and why I am here; I had to be patient.

To start, I walked around the house to have a look. Just behind there is a small wood I decided to enter; it is a mix of oak and birch (I think that is what the second type of tree is), and all the trees have already lost their leaves. They are not very tall, about three to five metres—up here tall trees would not survive the winds. In the woods the few dry grasses and brackens shy away because in there the kingdom belongs to the mosses—and the lichens too. Mosses have always fascinated me because it is as though you are never close enough to see all the detail—they appear to have micro–mosses on mosses in a never–ending fractal loop. There is no surface in the woods, vegetable or mineral (or animal if there were any sloths around here) that is not colonised either by mosses or by lichens (often both). This is their place, and if you want to grow here, you have to take them with you.

After some time looking around other of the wood's inhabitants noticed me; a couple of red grouse, and a running somebody (it was so efficient in its retreat that 'mammal' is as far as I can venture to guess). I felt like an intruder, so I went back to the field where reeds and short green grasses did not seem to mind me. I then realised that the sun's rays were already touching the tip of the cottage's chimney. I thought I would take a note of the time (10:25 a.m.).

It took me about an hour to get to the next village. Once there I looked for a telephone box I saw marked on the map—I just wanted to know where it was in case I had an emergency. I found it, I picked up the phone to see if it worked, and I could hear the tone. In the display, though, a message saying that cash was not accepted puzzled me—no cards slot either. I decided I would deal with the mystery only if I ever need to use this phone.

On the way to the village I came across the sea, a small loch, some hills, and plenty of sheep and cattle. All of them behaved very confidently and quietly. Ah, and one human being; an old toothless lady with a classic handkerchief covering her head. I said, 'Good morning', and she said, 'Hello'. That was it.

While I was walking I noticed again how low the sun was. At noon, when the sun reaches its highest point in the sky, it was still shining directly onto my face. I could completely cover it with my hand open and my arm fully extended, and still touch the horizon line with my thumb. I remember that when I was in Manaus, in the heart of the Brazilian Amazon, very close to the equator line, the sun was most of the time right above my head. It was literally impossible to walk under the shade of buildings, since no object cast any shadow at all. Here, it is quite the opposite. Today at noon I measured my own shadow and it was 21 steps long. Before or after noon it would have been even longer! Funny things happen on this purple planet.

On my way back I passed a house with a sheepdog on the other side of the fence looking intensely towards me. I did not remember seeing the dog before, on my way to the village, and I was surprised he did not bark. When I got closer, the dog proceeded to follow me until the fence that separated us prevented him from going further. There was no barking, no tail wagging, and no display of teeth; he just looked straight at me.

I kept walking because I did not want to awaken his territorial duties, but after a while I heard some noise behind me. I turned around and, from the distance, I saw two dogs running straight towards me. They belonged to the same breed, and the smaller one was the one I had met a few minutes earlier.

Not for a moment did I think that they were going to attack me. I waited, and when they reached me they both jumped all over me in a very typical canine greeting fashion. I responded in accordance and, I do not know why, presumed then that the biggest dog had helped the smallest one to escape his fence. I kept walking and they, very excited, followed along with me. Not long after that I heard a human male voice calling a name—I do not remember what name, though. I indicated to the dogs that they were wanted by their pack leader, and I could see the younger dog beginning to go through a dilemma. The older dog, on the other hand, did not seem to understand the situation. From a distance I saw the calling human walking towards us. I waited because

I did not want to create a diplomatic conflict. The calling continued, and the younger dog kept running half way towards his master, and then back to me; whereas the older did not make any attempt to show that he was listening.

When the human got to us I reassured his territorial status giving him a greeting and some phrase that showed I was a completely passive part in the incident. Eventually, the human managed to hold the older dog by the neck — not too roughly — and off they went back to where they came from. The younger one followed them, looking every now and then over his shoulder to see whether I was still there. I did not want to make the process more difficult so I kept walking until they could not see me any more.

On my way home I kept thinking about the dog incident. I kept saying to myself that the whole thing was no more than two sheepdogs trying to keep their flock together, but the thought that I had frustrated a successful escape of two oppressed animals played on my mind. If they had been British prisoners in 1940 occupied France, how would I have reacted? Well, it would have depended on the side I was on at the time. On what side am I? Am I in the resistance? Am I a collaborationist? Am I a German soldier? Perhaps I am only a sheep.

Back home I had a nice lunch and, although I felt a bit tired, I began writing about my day. I had to keep probing my head, I should not forget that I was not on holiday; nevertheless, I decided that I would go out to enjoy the sunset. It was 15:30 when the sun went behind the hill, so I went outside to watch the colour show. It was, as yesterday, already quite cold (a few hours before I had recorded as much as 15°C, but now it was 4°C); soon frost would be back from its tea break.

Yes, as I had expected, we also had a very beautiful sunset today. Despite the lack of clouds the light changes were amazing. It lasted about an hour, and it was as quiet as anything else around here is; a very gradual transformation from yellow to orange, finishing off with the omnipresent purple. Not even the sunset dares to be too dramatic — there must be a huge giant sleeping somewhere, whom nobody wants to awaken. Perhaps the real sunsets do not have dramatic clouds around; perhaps the sun up here wants to go quietly, and this is why it is taking it so long; perhaps it is a shy sun that blushes when caught sneaking out. I am not surprised; it is so far from here that it must feel totally out of place; popping out in the morning, sliding quietly on the horizon, and going away with its head down. I like this sun; I should invite it for dinner sometime.

Chapter Four
December 13th 2001

Today's morning routine was pretty much the same as yesterday's — a little bit more control in my actions, though, and a little bit more success in all of them. I am quickly becoming used to this life.

When the sun was up I went for a walk. Leaving the cottage I saw again that unidentified mammal running away — now I am pretty sure that it was a brown hare. This time I went to the castle and the coastline behind it. It is an old castle, totally in ruins — I was surprised at how big it was once I got there because from the cottage it looks tiny. A lonely sheep was sleeping in one of the grass patches at the base of the castle, and because she looked cute I took a photo of the scene. When I approached I realised that the moving bridge that would allow access to the castle itself — otherwise surrounded by water during high tide — was missing. How on earth did that sheep get up there then?

I kept walking, and then I saw a spectacular view; behind the castle there is a narrow piece of sea, and in the middle of it a tiny island. As usual, everything was governed by silence; the water hardly ever moved and few birds flew. I took my binoculars and I watched a family of mergansers swimming along nicely while being observed by a group of seagulls that were resting on the island. Negotiating the slippery surfaces of the rocks exposed by the low tide I walked towards the water. After some time I decided to sit down and experience the tranquillity—this time the silence did not scare me at all. I enjoyed the scenery; it did not lack anything relevant. It felt in perfect harmony with the stillness of the water, the blue sky and the low light; another beautiful day in a beautiful place.

Then, further along the cost, something moved on the rocks. It was another sheep—well, this is what I thought then, but I wonder now whether it was the same sheep I saw earlier. What was a sheep doing on her own among the shore rocks? There was no grass there, just limpets and algae. The sheep spotted me, and slowly tried to get out of the way; it was not easy to negotiate those rocks—not for me or for her. I approached her to see whether I could find any other reason for her being there, but I could not. She kept looking at me and going out of my way; but not rushing; taking it easy and showing control.

Something was moving on the water. At first it seemed like a piece of kelp briefly surfacing under the effects of soundless waves, but it did not show the rhythmic pattern you would expect if that had been the case. I used the binoculars but I could not see anything. Moving a little bit closer I looked again. There it was; this time I could see it clearly; a couple of otters playing in the water. I took my video camera and recorded them—I almost couldn't see them because of the distance. Trying not to make a sound I got even closer, but I was very bad at my amateurish stalking—up here, in Silenceland, not to make a sound is almost impossible.

Eventually, I decided to find a comfortable rock and sit on it—I hoped that by staying still the otters would reappear. I was looking for them when I saw a dark mark on the water, quite far from where I saw the otters last time; it looked as if something was under the water producing a long shadow. I followed it with the binoculars and eventually I saw the head of a common seal popping out; almost simultaneously the otters showed up again—I did not know who to look at, the seal or the otters. Beside them, in the sky, a golden eagle flew by. How much luckier can someone get!

Looking at all those creatures I felt totally at peace with the world. I was glad I was quite far from them, because I did not want to interrupt their wild life. I felt an intense sense of completeness. The rocks, the island, the fauna, the flora, the sun, all could have been part of a scene from thousands of years ago, before humans ever reached these lands. I was so lucky I had managed to leap in time and have a peek. It was right; it was good; it was perfect.

It did not last long, though. Two dark figures crossed the sky at high speed, one slightly above and behind the other. Their sound joined their images; two RAF jets in training, again—a total anticlimax. At first the animals seemed not to bother, but when the jets were gone a seagull that was resting on the small island uttered a long and high–pitched call that sounded like a profound lament. I looked around and all the animals had gone, including the mysterious sheep. Some other gulls joined the first in its call, and I wanted to join them too. I remembered that behind the rocks the ruins of a castle proved that human war had already reached this land hundreds of years ago. The jets showed me that it had never left them. Saddened, I went back home; it was time to write.

I have now written what I have seen; what I have felt. I have been doing it since I arrived, but I still do not know what I have to write about. Is this what I am supposed to do? Is this book about my everyday experiences alone in a cottage? I do not think so.

I have done what my instinct has told me. I have stopped my work and I have come to the Highlands. I am here now, on my own, with no contact with the rest of the world. I know I am in the right place, I know that I am in the right time, but I do not know anything else. Is this what I have to do, get up in the morning, go for a walk, see some sheep, and then write about it? I have not complained yet. The cottage is wonderful and the sights are fantastic, but I came here to write, not to enjoy myself.

What is the point of writing this ranting, anyway? Maybe I am starting to suffer some sort of withdrawal symptoms. After all, it has been quite a change of lifestyle. Maybe the silence is getting into me. Although I live alone in Brighton I work at home with the TV always on—I guess it keeps me company. In fact, I even use it as my alarm clock, so there is not a single moment that I am in my flat without having a voice talking in the background. When I am zoo checking I often stay in B&Bs, and I always turn on the TV to feel relaxed; and if I am working abroad, then I am too busy to even miss the TV.

Thinking about it, though, it is funny how TV prevents us from perceiving the world we have around us. Do not misunderstand me, I do like TV—in fact I am addicted to it. I like it because it is a window to thousands of worlds, but I do recognise that it is biased towards any world but the real one. When the TV is on, the crack in the ceiling is not there any more, the bird singing by your window loses its voice, and the wonderfully mysterious shape of the wooden cutting board marks becomes invisible. No, it is not the evil of technology; if instead of TV you have a group of people telling you about their day the effect would be the same. On the other hand, remove people, remove TV, remove the radio...and then the crack becomes a valley, the bird becomes a musician, and cutting board marks become a weeping troll. It is a matter of attention.

We evolved in a three–dimensional world full of subtleties, not in a one–dimensional reality of ready–cooked stories. The stories free us from the struggles of everyday life, but also pull us away from the beauty of it. Here, on the island, I will not have this problem.

Maybe this is what I need to do; read into the subtleties of real life. Maybe I should go around the house and look, listen, see the things I would not normally see. Maybe I will have an answer if I do that. I have not explored all the rooms yet; I have not looked into all the drawers. I am going to do that.

Chapter Five
December 14th 2001

I cannot believe what happened yesterday evening. I was going around the cottage looking at paintings, browsing through old books and checking out all the corners I had not seen before, when in one of the rooms I suddenly felt uncomfortable. In between the kitchen — where I spend most of the time — and the toilet there is a hall that has the stairs to the bedrooms, and then a room that could be best described as a sitting room. It is in this room where I felt weird; this is the weird room.

It has a chimney, a blue sofa, a couple of armchairs, a tall round table with a lamp on it and some shelves with old books and dusty board games. On top of the fireplace there is a framed print of a stag hunted by two dogs. The stag looks frightened and the dogs look angry; the words 'The Stag at Bay' are written under the image. On the mantelpiece there is a deformed black and white picture of two old ladies walking among snow carrying two enormous piles of branches of some sort; by the picture there is a piece of coral, a pelvis from some creature, a long feather and a small horseshoe. Opposite the sofa there is a window with tacky blue curtains made of a dusty old fabric. On the windowsill, a metal plate holds a mixture of objects; an empty 'Scottish Bluebell' matchbox, several seashells, a calcite stone, an old tin candleholder and a partially eroded ram horn.

I have never stopped before in that room, despite the fact that is on the way to the toilet. It is too cold; I keep it closed, to prevent loosing the heat generated in the rest of the cottage.

As I was saying, when I was browsing through that room I felt a strange presence. After dark I tend to draw all the curtains in the part of the cottage I use, but I do not draw the ones in that room. Because of that I sensed a presence at the window, as if somebody was looking at me from outside. I looked through the glass and I thought I saw something moving. I was a bit alarmed, so I could not leave the event unchecked; I had to see what it was.

First, I tried to keep very still and listen. If there was somebody he or she would probably make some noise, but because I could not hear anything I went upstairs to pick up my torch. I took my jacket and I built up the courage to go out and confront whoever was there — I was aware that I had to find an explanation because I could not afford to have unresolved situations in my head that could be playing tricks on me later on. I was going to be alone in this place for quite a long time, so I should pull myself together and face whatever I had to face.

It was quite cold, but I do not think all the shaking came from the low temperature. I tried to see whether there was any switch that would turn on a light outside, but none seemed to have that effect. I opened the two doors that lead to the porch where the wood is kept, and then I opened the outside door—the lock is very rusty and does not open easily, so I guess it's a little bit more difficult at night, with the frost.

When I got outside I felt the intense dry cold of the northern night; no wind or breeze whatsoever. I used my torch and proceeded looking around—I was a bit nervous, the sound of my own steps on the ice made me jump a couple of times. I could not see anything; I could not see anyone.

I went to have a look under the weird room window and I pointed the torch to the floor. I saw some prints; some animal prints. On close examination they resembled sheep prints—well, I was almost sure they were sheep prints, I can tell the difference between a sheep print and a deer print.

Was that what I saw from the room? A sheep moving around my cottage at night. How can any sheep jump the fence that separates the cottage from the fields? Perhaps that print was old, from a sheep that had walked about months ago; but that could not be, because the prints had broken the frost underneath; those prints were not frozen; they had been produced recently.

Because I was getting really cold I went back in, straight into the kitchen, my own safe territory. What was going on? Was I being paranoid? Perhaps it was perfectly possible for a highland sheep to jump over fences in the middle of the night. Perhaps the light attracted her, as if she were a giant woolly moth. Look at that sheep in the castle, or that one on the shore rocks; they were doing things that did not make sense to me, were they not?

I also had to consider seriously the possibility that, after three days of sensory limitation, my brain was compensating for the lack of daily stimuli I was accustomed to with some of its own made–up images and sounds. Perhaps I had been underestimating the effect of a sudden change of planet. The best thing I could do was to go to bed, and see how I felt in the morning.

Today I woke up a little bit later than the other days, maybe because I was a little bit restless during the night. Funnily enough I was awoken by a sound; the sound of hollow metal being gently hit by dry bone; the sound of cowbells. I got up and looked through the window. The cottage was surrounded by cattle, with their long hair and cool attitude.

I dressed up and went outside. Yes, cattle all over the place — this time, though, on the right side of the fence. They behaved as normal cattle do, eating grass and looking at me with a mixture of curiosity and mistrust — nothing mystical in the event. I went all around the house to check whether there was any section of the fence that could explain the sheep incident, but none could. The whole perimeter was not only intact, but also no section seemed as though a sheep could have jumped over it. No trace of any sheep sleeping anywhere either.

I went back to examine the prints and to see whether I could track the steps. They were almost gone; I could hardly see them now, and I could definitely not trace them back anywhere. I had an explanation, though. Today, for the first time, there were some clouds in the sky. A very thin layer of clouds, but evenly distributed all over. Also, the temperature was much warmer and all the frost had gone. This made sense because around here, in the Atlantic, the Gulf Stream that comes from tropical Earth passes close by on its winter journey towards more northern latitudes. The clouds indicated that some air from the sea had reached us today, probably warmer air coming from the famous stream. This, in turn, had melted the frost earlier than usual, and since I was up later than usual the frost had gone. Yesterday's prints were on a mixture of frost, grass and mud. The frost had gone, the grass had stretched, and the only remaining evidence was the mud. That small part of the mystery had been resolved easily.

My renewed confidence in my deductive powers makes me feel much more relaxed about the whole thing, especially after having written about it. I think that, whatever the sheep incident was, I should use it. If it was either a real mysterious sheep checking me out, or just the fruits of partial sensory deprivation, the result of my experience about it could be interesting—I could make this the subject of my writing while I am waiting for the real one.

***

The cattle are still around the cottage, and because it is already sunset this is not normal. They have not moved for the whole day. Usually, cattle start eating grass somewhere and then move along. They did not; besides, I cannot hear their bells any more; in fact, none of the cows I can see now wears any bell.

Another strange thing happened today. I went to

the furthest room of the cottage—a room I never go to because it is inhabitable due to some construction work still needed—and I found a dead rabbit under a chair. How could a rabbit get into the cottage? It did not die that long ago because although it smelled of rotten flesh it was still quite intact. Maybe it entered the cottage a long time ago, died, got frozen, and since I arrived the heat defrosted it. It seemed the most plausible explanation, so I took it outside and I forgot about it—the hooded crows would probably eat it.

All day, because of the clouds, it has been darker than usual. I would not say it is very cold, but the whole atmosphere is oppressing. I feel as if the whole world is watching me; I do not like surprises, and I sense one coming soon.

It is going to be like last night, isn't it? I will be around, I will hear or see something, paranoia will grow, and I will feel intense exposure. OK, I must calm down; I must think rationally. It is obvious that since I have arrived here I have not been able to understand everything as I usually do. It is also clear that I have been suddenly deprived of my daily dose of broadcast information, and this could lead to some withdrawal symptoms. Also, my whole routine has changed to the smallest detail, and do not forget the well–known psychological effect of short days. Put all this together and it perfectly explains the occurrence of paranoia and feelings of exposure; besides, I am really exposed up here, this is a fact; exposed to the elements, exposed to unscrupulous humans that may have spotted my foreignness to the land, and exposed to myself.

Having identified the possible problems I need to see now whether I can find the right solutions. Let's assume that the paranoia is inevitable. How do I deal with it? How do I minimise its damaging effect? Well, as with all fears and phobias the best solution tends to be facing your ghosts. How can I do that? What are my ghosts here? Are they the cattle, the mysterious sheep? I am not sure.

Perhaps the answer will be in the weird room. Now that it is already dark I should go into that room and sit in one of the chairs. Perhaps I should even turn the lights off — if I dare; perhaps not, just sit there, and look around for a while; take some warm clothes, sit, and do nothing. Maybe it's a silly idea; maybe I should stay here and continue writing — maybe not.

I am going to do it.

Chapter Six
December 15th 2001

Nothing will ever be as it was before. It looks just like any other morning, but it is not. I cannot tell you how happy I was to see the sun rising. I do not even know how to start; well, I'd better start from the beginning.

I went into the weird room determined to get to the bottom of whatever was worrying me. I sat in one of the armchairs, the one that faces the fireplace and the stag picture on top of it. It is a funny looking armchair. It is sort of orange and has this tall back and arms, so when you sit on it you feel sunk into it. On the left, the tall round table seems very unpractical — too high from that chair.

I sat there for some time, looking at the paintings, the window and the old books. I spotted what appeared to be a photo album. I stood up and took it from the shelves. It was full of drawings, paper articles, photos, poems, and people's signatures. Many of the pictures showed the cottage, most of them with people painting its walls. There were also pictures and drawings of animals of all kinds: the head of a cat, a dolphin jumping and a dog very similar to the sheepdog I saw few days ago. Most of the dates written were late sixties and early seventies.

An article in particular drew my attention. In it, there was an image of a wasp attacking a bee; the legend read: "Before taking it back to the nest, a worker wasp dismembers a honeybee, leaving inedible parts behind."

The browsing of that album had relaxed me. It made me realise that this cottage had been full of life, and had probably generated plenty of happiness. An air of nostalgia radiated from it. Just like me, many people had abandoned their busy lives to find temporary retreat in here. I did not feel out of place anymore; I definitely felt calmer.

Encouraged by my improved confidence I decided to take my experiment a step further. I decided to turn the lights off and immerse myself into the mystery of the room; so I did. In complete darkness I found my way back to the orange armchair, and sat in silence.

There was no fear, no apprehension. My mind comfortably wandered through various images that disappeared as quickly as they appeared; like butterflies that never stop flying, my thoughts never stopped moving, so I could not catch any of them.

Then I heard a noise; a faint creak. I thought it could be mice; I had not seen any yet in the cottage but I had assumed they were present because I found their droppings in the toilet area. I had concluded earlier that the droppings were old—probably from the summer—and the lack of inhabitants and heat had got rid of the mice—I supposed I was wrong, and they had come back.

I heard another creaking sound somewhere else in the room and I thought that I had to have a proper look. I stood up and, in the dark, I found my way to the light switch. When I turned it on my heart almost stopped.

I do not know whether I should continue writing this. Maybe this is not right and I should keep the whole thing secret. Perhaps this is not a good idea; perhaps I will be violating some important cosmic law of some kind if I write my experience.

You must believe that I have gone mad, that I have lost it. You may be right. I am going to eat something, and think of what to do.

***

My stomach is quiet now, the kitchen is quite warm, and I will have no need to go to the toilet for quite a while. I know now that my experience has something to do with my book, and therefore it has to be written; it has to be written in detail, I do not care if it sounds mad. This is what is happening to me, either inside or outside. I do not care.

When I turned the lights on in the weird room I realised I was not the only one in it anymore. On the sofa, the armchairs, the table, the mantelpiece and every available space in the room there was somebody else.

I could not breathe. With my hand still on the light switch I froze completely. My eyes were going through all their faces, one after another. I could feel my blood pulling away from my skin in retreat; my legs firmly nailed to the floor, my jaw permanently petrified. I could not believe my eyes; I could not believe that the room was full of animals.

Animals of all sorts; cats, monkeys, lizards, sheep, dogs, insects, apes, fish — you name it. All of them were sitting there, quietly. All of them were looking straight at me, straight at my shocked eyes.

Eventually, my brain made me breathe and I could see the condensation coming out of my mouth collecting on my glasses. I moved my hand away from the light switch, I took my glasses off and, shaking, I wiped them with my sleeve and put them back on. The animals were still there, not having moved a bit.

At that stage I could have gone through some sort of mental process trying to explain the phenomenon, but I did not. Overwhelmed by the illogically bizarre situation my brain refused to operate. Not knowing why, I proceeded walking towards the orange armchair, the only empty space in the entire room. I sat there, I kept looking, and I kept breathing.

Eventually, I dared a timid 'hello' — I always greet all animals I meet with a 'hello', it seems to work on all occasions, probably because they understand the intention. I was expecting a verbal reply or some equivalent — after all, if those animals could suddenly appear in the room they could well talk too. But they did not; they did not react to my voice at all.

I was totally tense. My back was not touching the armchair and my hands were in a fist — my back hurts right now while I am typing, I guess I must have pulled a muscle. I did not know what else to say. It was obvious I was facing some sort of paranormal experience, and I did not know what is the standard response to it, other than screaming and running away.

All the animals looked very normal to me. They looked real and, apart from the fact that they were sitting there and not moving, they behaved as they normally do. They did not have human expressions, nor did they make me think in any way that they were anything else than the animals they appeared to be; nevertheless, they had suddenly showed up from the dark, and were sitting there in the room—normal animals do not do that.

I was looking at their faces, and in doing so I sensed something; I felt that I was missing an important element. Each of their faces was telling me something, but I did not know what. Were they trying to communicate with me? Were they somehow trying to telepathically reach me? If so, I could not get the message. Something was in their faces, but I could not tell what; it was as a kind of déjà vu, or that feeling when you meet somebody that you have not seen for a long time, and you do not remember who they are. Yes, exactly, this is how it felt, and this is exactly what it was—I cannot stop weeping right now while I am writing this. Yes, I knew them all, each and every one of them. I knew them, and I had forgotten them. They were the animal people that I had met in my life. They were all back, they had come back from where they had been all these years. They all had names; they all had souls; they all knew me; I knew them all.

I have to leave it for a while; I do not think I can continue writing right now.

***

I am much calmer—I have to learn to control myself if I want to go through this. I feel that it is important that I never stop writing whatever happens, whatever I experience. This is the book, I feel it coming now, and this is why I came up here.

Here they all were; Chico, Django, Jordi, Vieja, Clyde, Tiao, Nuska...so many, all there, cramped in the weird room, surrounding me, waiting for me to do something, to say something.

I stood up and, weeping, I extended my hand to them. I walked through the room, touching them, stroking them; some reacted to me, many did not. They all felt real, as they were when I first met them.

My life had crossed the life of each and every one of them at one point in our past; in some cases briefly, in others as long as a whole life span. Some of them had been my friends; I had been the enemy of others. All of them went away before something could be said.

I sat by them, waiting for a signal, for the next step, but nothing else happened. I did not know what to do, and neither did they. I talked to them, but they did not respond. Nothing was happening; nothing at all.

A sense of responsibility fell on me, as if I had missed my cue, or I had forgotten the script; this developed into emptiness, and soon the situation seemed unbearable. I ran out of words, ideas, tears and patience, so I stood up, opened the door, and left the room. I ran upstairs, I locked myself in the bedroom, and stayed there, sleepless, until this morning. When the sun came out I went back downstairs, I opened the door, and they were gone.

I have not gone out today. I have been sat here, writing and writing. The sun is already somewhere else, and now I am facing the possibility that they may be back in the room. I cannot do anything else other than go back there; if they are back, this will be the last sentence for today.

Chapter Seven
December 16th 2001

I know how it works now; I understand what this is all about; it does not make complete sense yet but I know more or less how it works. From now on it is going to be as follows; after sunset the animals will return to the weird room and I will join them; after midnight I will go to sleep in the bedroom; after sunrise I will write about my experience with them the day before; and after sunset the cycle will be repeated.

I have realised that this entire situation is about me; I know that I have been called to face them; I know that there is much explaining to do. I have been to many places and I have done many things; some on my own, some with other people; some with human beings, many with non–human beings; some good, some bad; some important, some irrelevant. I have been called to explain them all, to say what I did, what I felt, and why I did them. I am being put on trial; I do not know who is the judge, the jury or the lawyers, but I am being put on trial, and I will go through it.

When I was sitting in the orange armchair I looked again at all their faces to see whether I could go a little bit further than the evening before. I stopped when I got to Nuska—she is a middle–aged dog, mixed breed between Greyhound and Alsatian; she has got one ear up and the other down, and she is pale brown all over her body. She was the first dog I ever had, when I lived with my parents in Barcelona.

They were strange times back then. Spain was under the dictatorship of an Army General, who was a nasty Fascist that did not like anyone that was not a pure Catholic right–winged Spaniard. My whole family was Catalan, as were most people in the Barcelona area, but our culture was suppressed then and we could not even speak freely our own language in public. Political turmoil was present everywhere; in the school, the church and on the street. I remember the day our school routine stopped to talk about the summary execution of an anarchist the day before. I remember when the car of the General's right hand man was blown up by the Basques, our brothers in the struggle. I remember when the 'grey people'—as we called the General's police—stormed into church due to a tip off about an illegal gathering. I remember that the number of rubber bullets children managed to collect was a measure of their status in the street.

Despite all that, I do not recall my childhood then as the worst period of my life. To start with, I did not understand what was going on, but also I was not deprived of many of the things children are supposed to have. These included, of course, the family pet. Ever since I can remember we had an albino cat, Titina, but getting a dog seemed a much bigger deal. I do not recall exactly how we got her, but she was an important part of my early childhood.

We lived in a small flat on the sixth floor of a not too old apartment building in an area called *Guinardo* — quite a working class quarter, far from Barcelona's city centre. We did not have a garden, just a little balcony of about three square metres completely covered with plants of all sorts. So, when Nuska wanted to go out, we either let her go to the balcony — and do what she needed to do there — or took her downstairs for a walk. The street was quite busy since it was a relatively important artery that linked several city areas, and for this reason we had to take Nuska on the lead all the time — she would have been easily run over by a car otherwise.

Like all dogs, she loved to go out, and she could always predict when we were thinking of taking her. We did not even need to say a word; she was at the door already wagging her tail. Once in the street we went around the block stopping at each plantain tree, where she would do her business. Well, I myself did not go all around the block because behind my building there was a badly reputed small hill where gypsies lived — I had already been bullied numerous times by them. Hence, the back of the building was out of bounds for me.

One summer — and I do not know why — became the luckiest of all. My parents managed to rent a small holiday apartment in a place called *La Floresta*. It was not on the beach or anything, but it was in the countryside — well, sort of. We had never been away on holiday before, so we all were very excited.

We shared this summerhouse with other members of my family, and I remember having a brilliant time — for a city boy even looking at ants' nests seemed amazing. All very nice and exciting, until one day we came back from an afternoon of running around and found that everybody at home had very serious expressions on their faces. My parents took us to another room and told us what had happened; Nuska had made a hole under the fence, had escaped and had been run over by a car, and her disembowelled body had been thrown into a quarry.

At first, I did not know how to react, but soon I began crying, like everyone else. The more I cried, the more I believed that this was not enough; I had to do something more. I took a comic book that was lying around and I tore it into pieces with my teeth. I ended up eating it, as many people that were present kept reminding me years later. Nobody stopped me.

After her death, and probably because I never saw her dead body, I used to dream about Nuska very often, even many years later. I used to dream that she would return, somehow, somewhere. She never did, until now.

I had not thought about her for many years, and here she was, in the weird room, with me. She broke the formation and approached me wagging her tail. A knot formed in my throat and my stomach shrank. I patted her as I used to do, trying to say hello with almost no voice. She seemed happy, she seemed well, but she was not. She died running, running for her freedom; running when she saw all those trees, many more than the plantains she used to have, many more than the plants on the balcony.

She never understood why she had to be on the lead, she never understood why sometimes we thought of taking her out and then we changed our minds. She never understood why we did not come when she was dying on the tarmac with her body ripped apart. She just wanted to be with us, and to run towards those trees.

I was a child then. I knew nothing about life and death. People were killing one another in the street, and I did not understand why. My dog ran away, I cried, and I ate a comic book. What else could I have done? I was not there. I did not know. I could not have done anything.

Nothing, nothing in there was my fault! I have nothing to be blamed for; I was a child, for Goodness sake! I was a child, and I loved her even after death!

I left the weird room and Nuska came with me. I opened the cottage door and, jumping about and wagging her tail, she ran away towards the trees until she disappeared into the darkness. She did not need the lead anymore; she had been on it for far too long.

Chapter Eight
December 17th 2001

L ast night I slept well, but this morning I was awoken again by the sound of cowbells; when I looked through the window to see whether the cattle were outside I could not see anyone anywhere. I blocked both my ears with my fingers and, to my astonishment, the sound was still there; not very loud, but still there, somewhere in my head—this explains a lot, don't you think?

Today is also a cloudy warm day; the clouds are thicker than yesterday's, but more patchy, and the temperature is about four degrees Celsius. I have finished my first milk carton; it has lasted as I planned, which made me believe that I will not run out of provisions. My laptop was playing funny games when I turned it on; some system failures that have been thankfully corrected with the normal diagnostic tools—as long as the computer keeps its feet on the ground, we'll be OK. I forgot to comment that among the deprivations I imposed on myself on this journey caffeine is one of them. I do drink tea here, but it is decaffeinated. I just thought that this piece of information could help you to understand things that go on up here—cowbells and all that.

I feel somehow released today. In a strange way the oddness of my experiences seems to follow a logical pattern. I am a little bit more in control of this surreal world. It is not bizarre, it is surreal; it is somehow real, but on a different plane, on a plane above the one I normally live on. It is not like a dream, full of random events and broken sequences; it is another world with its own little rules.

While I have been writing I have noticed that the tree close to the cottage, which can be seen through the kitchen window, is full of birds; blackbirds, blue tits, chaffinches, great tits, greenfinches, redstarts, dunnocks, fieldfares, you name it. All jumping around from branch to branch, chasing one another, pecking things on the grass, cleaning their feathers—you know, bird stuff. I cannot hear any singing or calling, though, but bear in mind I am inside the cottage and the laptop hurricane is full on.

Opposite the main cottage entrance, among dried and dead plants of all sorts, a group of short leafless trees creates what could be described as a mini–wood—it is obvious that before this was a garden but now it has gone wild. This former garden, now unattended, proudly belongs to Mr Robin, as he kindly reminds me, with his confident showing off, every day I pass by. Perhaps this morning he organised a bird party of some kind; maybe today is Sunday, and this is a regular gathering.

Chaffinches seem to dominate in number, but blue tits are the ones that draw much of my attention; they occasionally fly close to the window and have a peek inside. I can hear now some hooded crows from the distance — they must be complaining because they have not been invited.

I can feel you are not interested in the birds. You want to know what happened last evening, don't you? You do not want to hear about birds, trees, or pints of milk. You want to know what happened after I wrote Nuska's story.

Yes, night came on time, and so did they.

In the weird room, nervously looking at me as they used to do about six years ago, Jordi and Georgina, the two common marmosets (a type of very small South American monkey) had caught my eye. They had a rough time, poor chaps.

During a period of my life, while deeply involved in my investigation on the international illegal primate trade, I travelled quite a lot. I had managed to adapt quite well to the life of downtown Manaus — in the heart of the Brazilian Amazon — with its hot humid climate, common petty crime and rough commercial crowds. In there, as in anywhere else in the world, one of the best ways to get good information is to chat with people while having a drink.

I had just met a chap from Guyana who was looking for 'gringos' to befriend — this is a common way to get some money from them — so after the second ice cold beer — it is either ice cold or warm in Brazil — you could say that the conversation was quite fluid. Knowing my interest in primates he mentioned that he had seen a couple of Spanish tourists who had managed to buy two marmosets from the black market, and were intending to smuggle them to Europe. He did not remember their names nor their hotel, but after some economic persuasion he told me that they wanted to go to visit the army zoo — the Brazilian army owned a zoo, where animals, allegedly, had been used for jungle 'training'.

Next day I went to the army zoo to see whether or not I was going to be lucky. Sure enough, as with everything else on that, my first — but not last — trip to Brazil, luck stayed with me all the way; there, in the distance, doing something to a cat, I saw a couple that looked foreign to me. Making some baby noises she was playing with a jaguar through the bars while he was taking pictures of the scene; they seemed very young, early twenties, or even less. I approached casually and I noticed they were speaking in Spanish — with a distinctive Basque accent, by the way.

Pretending to be a fellow tourist it was not difficult to introduce myself to them. We spent the day together, as you do, and later in the evening, after a few drinks, they asked me if I wanted to see something 'cute'. They took me to their hotel room, opened the door, turned the lights on, and pointed towards the bed. On it there was a small grey hairy mass that seemed to move; two baby marmosets, no more than 3 inches tall, and no more than 40 days or so old, were tumbling about; later I found out they were brother and sister.

They had been bought illegally ($30 each) at a street market in *Salvador*, on the Brazilian east coast. They had travelled miles in a tiny wicker basket, by coach to the mouth of the Amazon River, and from there to Manaus on a five day boat trip. They were dehydrated, malnourished and hypothermic. They had been fed with leftovers, when they still needed their mother's milk. The next day they were going to be squashed into the tiny basket again, taken to the airport, flown to Spain on a more than ten hour flight, and in the unlikely event they survived the trip, spend the rest of their fragile life as pets in somebody's bedroom.

Trying to control myself by being as diplomatic as possible I pointed out to the couple that the marmosets did not look good at all. They seemed surprised; they had no idea they were babies, they thought they were adults. I believe them; as I suspected the couple were just kids, one 19 and the other 20, and they did not know much about anything, let alone primates. Although they understood the babies were not well, and that they should be fed with milk rather than leftovers and be kept warm at all times, they were still adamant to smuggle them to Spain.

I had no choice other than to come out of my cover and tell them that I was working for a British organisation investigating the illegal primate pet trade. I told them that if they were going to stick to their plan I would not have any other alternative than to denounce them to the police. After some panic and a lot of talking we arrived at a deal. I would give them until the next morning to think about it, and after that if they handed over the marmosets to me I would not denounce them to the police.

Very early in the morning I was waiting outside their hotel when the boy came out to check that there were no surprises waiting for them. He saw me and gave me a signal. They both came outside with their luggage, I approached them and, almost without looking at me, they passed me the tiny basket. I could see she had tears in her eyes.

I let them go and I rushed into my hotel, which luckily was close by. I opened the basket and after taking a quick photo I took both marmosets out. They were very cold, and they began screaming as soon as they saw me — a very high–pitched scream. In their mind their real parents were still out there so they were hoping they would return to rescue them at any time — if they screamed loud enough. In those days I had very long hair, so I put both marmosets on my head to allow them to hold on to it — as they would do with their parents — and get warm with my body heat. Keeping them on my head would also give me free movement, as well as discretion because nobody would see them entangled among my brown hair. I went to the street to make some phone calls, and eventually I managed to talk to somebody I had been working with for years in the business of rescuing and rehabilitating primates from the pet trade. I trusted this man; I had been working very closely with him, and perhaps he could look after the marmosets.

With both monkeys still in my hair I took a taxi to my friend's place. Once there we weighed them (one was 61 grams the other 71 grams, I still remember) and we fed them with baby milk and mealworms. It seemed as though they would make it, but it was too early to tell.

Knowing that my friend would do as much as possible to keep them alive and well I left them with him and came back to town to resume my work. Next morning I met my friend somewhere else; he was carrying one of the marmosets whom, in my honour, he had baptised with the name 'Jordi'. The other never made it through the night. In my mind she received the name of 'Georgina'.

I went back to Brazil several times, and I saw Jordi grow up and become a parent. But he never made it back to the wild. All my Brazilian friend's plans to create a primate rehabilitation centre—where monkeys such as Jordi could be taken back to a natural life—were tangled in such a bureaucratic jungle that Jordi did not make it. He died a couple of years ago.

I sat there in the weird room trying to figure out which one was Jordi and which one was Georgina. They looked very much the same, as when I rescued them. I extended my hand and I tried to put them on my head, despite the fact that now my hair is considerably shorter. One of them did climb on it, but the other did not; it refused to climb, and instead made a small alarm squeak and came back to where it was sitting before. Its characteristic twitching stopped, and its eyes focused directly into mine. That one was Jordi; I could recognise him now.

Yes, I know I rescued them, but from what? Rescued from the bad tourist?—they were not bad, just young and naïve. Rescued from the evil animal dealers?—it was too late for that; they already had been sold on the black market, and not because the dealers were evil, but because the tourist had money. Rescued from their empty life as family pets?—they never would have made it through the Atlantic. Rescued from a premature death, perhaps?

I rescued them for me; to feel good about myself; to feel I had done something; to have my own name given to the survivors in my 'honour'—in my honour? A few months later, in the comfort of a cosy evening in front of the fire, I was in my home in Cornwall explaining my adventures to my housemates. Meanwhile, the other Jordi began learning that his cage was 'as good as it gets'; and millions of other Jordies ended up, after all, in somebody's bedroom as pets—in my honour?

Georgina climbed onto my head because I helped her to avoid the cold, and at least to die warm. Jordi did not because I was responsible for his long life in captivity. What is this, a draw? One–one, next game! No, it does not work like this. Helping an old lady to cross the street does not give you an extra point that gets you closer to the amount you need to buy a guilt–free murder.

Ethics is not a matter of arithmetic; it is a matter of actions and judgements. Georgina does not judge me because of what I did to Jordi in the long run, nor indeed in the short run. She judges me for what I did to her in the very short run. In fact, she does not even judge me really, she just remembers me as a giant blanket, and I have not done anything to contradict her memories. Jordi should judge me in the same way, and therefore conclude that his captivity had nothing to do with me. Why didn't he?

On the other hand, if I judge my own actions retrospectively, I can see how I created a captive animal by preventing it dying in the hands of the naïve—and therefore innocent—tourists. The point is that, although I can now see the result of my actions, I could not see it when I took them. As far as my judgement six years ago is concerned, my actions could have concluded in two healthy marmosets returning to the wild, who, otherwise, would have died in pain. How could an action that was taken six years ago in good judgement turn out to be wrong six years later? Wasn't 'Good' supposed to be timeless?

Perhaps that action was always right. If today, with my knowledge of the affairs of things, I was presented with the same situation, would my actions be different? Would I let the marmoset be smuggled today? Probably not, because my hope of being able to return them back to the wild has not vanished, and therefore the possibility that my actions may lead to a greater good justifies them.

This is true, but considering that my present knowledge also tells me that the probability of returning them successfully is small, the fact that the possibility of doing it still exists is not enough to justify my actions. This remote possibility can equally justify the most terrible crimes, like murdering somebody in order to prevent a 'possible' worse death.

No, the possibility of helping is not a good reason for help. Your actions must be likely to help, and likely to help soon, if they have to be taken under a responsible moral judgement. If I were presented with the same situation today, I would do the same, because that would help both Jordi and Georgina in the short run, providing them with warmth and food. My knowledge about the future consequences is overridden by my knowledge about the immediate ones, because my moral judgement is designed to work in the short term, in order to keep me alive and gather more friends than enemies.

On top of that, my actions that lead to Jordi's captivity were not at the cost of his freedom. He had already been caught and sold before I met him, so without my intervention he might have survived and ended up alone as a pet in a Spanish house, rather than in the company of other marmosets in a Brazilian cage, as he did. Is that not another positive outcome of my actions?

According to all this, Jordi should have climbed onto my head, but he did not. What is wrong? What did I do wrong?

I looked at Jordi again in the weird room, and when I tried to pick him up he continued refusing. I kept staring at him, not understanding where my logic went wrong. He scratched himself a couple of times and proceeded grooming his tail. He behaved calmly, much more maturely that Georgina did. He seemed knowledgeable and aware of things I did not know.

I often have this feeling when I look at animals. When I stare deep into any adult animal's eyes I do not see questions, I only see answers. The trouble is that I am unable to read those answers. It is as if we, humans, are a species strangled by a question mark. I think this is a by–product of evolution, which made us carry a big brain designed to ask but poorly equipped to give answers.

There are no answers that satisfy us. We want to know more and we always have a hundred questions lined up. We have so many questions, that we do not even listen to the answers, as if they are irrelevant or unimportant. We base our science, religion, education, art, philosophy, and anything else we see as typically human on unanswered questions. Who created the world? Where is the missing link? Who were the Celts? Is there an afterlife? Is AIDS curable? Why did this artist paint this? Whom should we vote next time? Do you want to marry me? Do you really want to marry me? To be, or not to be...

When it is the turn of answers then we do not know any. We do not know how to deal with our lives, with our families, with our countries, with our species or with our planet. We just do not have a clue. Look what we are doing to the world. It is very likely that our questioning brain will be what will extinct us, but ironically our only hope may be the same question mark that is strangling us. Our only escape may be by jumping from the cliff of ignorance.

Most animals I know do not have these problems, though. You look at their eyes and you do not see question marks. They know what they are doing; they know what they are supposed to know; but this only works with adult animals because when you look at baby animals, there are question marks everywhere. They are still learning, you see; we are the ones that never grow up.

I then realised my mistake. I then realised why Jordi did not climb into my hair; he was not a baby any more. He was an adult, he had survived, and he had seen me as an adult when I went every year back to Brazil. He had seen me coming, and he had seen me going away. He had seen me leaving him in his cage; abandoning him there; that's why. It is not what I did to him by rescuing him, but what I did not do when I saw him spend the rest of his life in a cage. Nothing to do with my cheap philosophical arguments about judgements and actions, but with the simple fact I did not return him to the life he deserved.

I let Georgina climb down from my hair and go with her brother; she climbed on his back. She looked safe.

Chapter Nine

December 18th 2001

Today I decided to go for a walk. I have not gone out for two or three days now and I think it is time to move away from the cottage for few hours. I need to feel the connection with Nature again; I need to feel that I understand it, that I remember it, that I sense it. I need to feel I have learnt something from it, not only about it. It is not a cold day—four degrees Celsius again—and there are plenty of clouds around, but none seem particularly threatening. I'll eat my porridge, I'll drink my tea, I'll get my boots on, and I'll go—I have to remember to take some food with me this time, an apple or so.

* * *

I'm back, and I feel quite refreshed; I needed it, after yesterday's session. I have been walking along the north–west hills of moorland, on the very edge of the sea. I went back to the point where I saw the otters the other day, but they must have been somewhere else today. Most of the seagulls stayed put on the small island, which they seem to share happily with a group of polite cormorants — or were they shags? I am not sure. The sea water was going south, returning to the ocean, and there was a slight breeze.

It's a fine place, this purple planet — yes, still purple, more than ever. It is not just the frost and the light that makes it purple. Take, for instance, the rocks. I have been examining them closely, and most rocks up here are composed of some sort of sandstone that gives them a pale reddish colour; on top of them, many types of lichen grow, but there is one in particular, quite common, that has a light bluish tone. Well, from a distance, the pale reddish mixes with the light bluish, and the rock looks purple.

Take the trees, for example. All the trees up here have no leaves, and therefore is difficult to tell what is what, but in all of them the grey of the branches against the blue sky insinuates some purple tones. Apart from oaks, every now and then you can find patches of small trees — I think they are some sort of birch — that look very purple even when seen from a short distance; if you get even closer you can see that the bark is also reddish, but with paler bands and darker buds which help to create the purple colour. Not to mention the heather with its flowers. If you put all these together in a place where the sunrays have to cross a particularly thick part of the atmosphere — and therefore the resulting light tends to be slightly refracted — you will have a purple planet.

Despite the fact that I am getting used to this landscape I am still amazed how different things are here — I am going to keep calling it a planet, if you don't mind. For example, today I was walking through the moors. When you walk on the planet I used to live, you just walk, looking every now and then at the ground trying to avoid stones and puddles; you find the flattest and most uniform surface, and you go through it. On this planet, it does not work like this. Here, if you follow that logic, you will end up in a pit—and perhaps never be found again. On this moory planet, you see, water, holes, mud, streams, ditches and all sort of obstacles you normally try to avoid are scattered all over the place, but at the same time are skilfully camouflaged. At first, it appears that there is no pattern; what seems solid is sometimes solid, but sometimes is not; what seems dry sometimes is dry, but sometimes not. After trial and error, some sort of pattern begins to emerge. When you see dry grass in a prominent place, usually it is solid; when you see heather, almost certainly it is solid; when you see a flat surface that could be a path, and has lots of moss on it, normally it is full of water.

After you have been walking around and you have already figured out that the best way to move is to do almost the opposite of what you would do on your home planet—avoid flat surfaces that look like pathways or horizontal planes, or go to the left if you want to go to the right—that is when your confidence will ditch you into a pit—and believe me, in some of them you can even hear the sound of kangaroos leaping about. Why? Because that is when you will face the exception to the rule—on this planet, the exception is as common as the rule, hence the alien logic.

There is always a way to master any harsh terrain, though. Here, it is not the Land Rover, or the hovercraft;

here, it is the walking stick—not that typical old person one, but the taller one, stronger and specially cut for the task. With the stick, you always can check your intuition before your foot goes, and that is when you learn about the Highlands logic. Once you master the stick, you can go anywhere. Oh yes, the Highland moors, where NASA astronauts should be training—better not.

I found myself getting proficient in the art of moor walking. It was as if I were blind, and I needed the stick for each and every step I was going to make; but this is how it has to be, because every time my mind drifted away and I paid less attention to the moor, the stick found an unexpected hole.

In an odd way, I experienced a little bit how it would feel to be blind. Sometimes our lives are so loud and shiny that it seems impossible to open our eyes. Only the blind, or otherwise visually impaired, can open them. Maybe through their stick they can perceive what we cannot see. Maybe because they cannot see into the distance, and their attention is focused on the immediate reality around them, they are less likely to get lost.

Another amazing thing about the moors is that all the moss, heather and grass has the effect of cushioning everything. It is not just that they make the rocks, by comparison, feel more solid—after having walked for a while on the spongy *Sphagnum* moss, emergent rocks seem islands of dry gravity—but also these plants absorb all possible sounds. This morning I found a small stream that produced no sound at all, even when I put my ear at about a foot from the water; the rocks are so smooth, and the moss absorbs so much of the impact of the water, that no splashes occur.

Today I needed a little bit of old fluffy purple planet. Yesterday's session was not particularly good. I suppose I cannot avoid any longer telling you about it. It is getting darker now, so I better hurry up, or I am going to miss the next one.

There was somebody sitting on top of the mantelpiece, just under the stag picture. I was not sure who it was. I stood up, and holding my glasses near to my eyes, I got a little bit closer. Ah, Ana, that was Ana the white rat.

I did my first degree in Zoology in one of the universities in Barcelona, in the early 1980s. At that time, the degree was composed of two parts, the first three years when you would become a Biologist, and the last two years when you would become a Zoologist. So, the first three years were the same for everybody who was going to be working in any biological subject — Botanist, Geneticists, Biochemists, Ecologist, Zoologist, etc.

There is something dangerous about Science. When you have to produce scientists as you produce sausages, it is likely that rather than scientists you will produce technicians. I have always considered myself a scientist because of my inquisitive attitude to life, my urge to make sense of this world through reason, and my interest in persuading others through logic. These kinds of things are not normally taught in universities, at least the ones I know. Instead, what we are taught are techniques of how to deal with scientific queries, and how to standardise practices so that we can all harmoniously fit into the never–stopping big machine of academia. In other words, it seems more important to create perfect machine parts that heartlessly follow the rules, than emotional souls that tend to break them. In other words; technicians, or even worse, technocrats.

The process of transforming a young emotional teenager into a cold controlled technician takes some time and effort, and the universities I know do not want to waste this time. It appears to be more efficient to pre–select people that will go through the transformation swiftly, than to try to tame an over–sensitive human being. At my university, in the early 1980s, this pre–selection seemed to occur in the second year. During that year, all students, regardless which branch of Biology they would eventually take, had to perform a ritual that in my opinion was specifically designed to deal with emotions — despite the fact nobody would admit this, not even today. After the ritual, some students would look for another career, others would struggle to continue, and others would open themselves to the possibility of learning to do things they never thought capable of doing.

This ritual involved the decapitation of a live rat. You had to wear your white coat, learn to pick up the rat, learn to make it sleep, and then cut its head off, using a blade, by hand. No matter how much you protested, or how much you demanded a justification for it; if you did not do it, that would be the end of your degree — even if your intention was to study arctic lichens.

The system worked, because those who were too emotionally involved to become efficient technicians tended to quit as a consequence of the experience, and those who had some doubts learned to see the power of goals over means. Yes, I do have a degree in Zoology, so you know what this means.

Do you really want to know what I felt? Do you really want to know how it felt? Do you really want me to tell you how bad I was at it, and how long it took me? I will spare you all that.

I did resist; I did talk to the lecturers; I did try to find a way out.

Afterwards, I did my best to raise awareness, and I did campaign, with others, for the abolition of such an horrendous ritual. After years of protests, we eventually managed, at least, to make that practice voluntary (I am not aware whether or not this practice is still performed or how widespread it was among other universities in Europe). All my protests and ignorance, though, did not help Ana, nor the millions of Anas that, since then, might have had the chance to know that their executioners have free will.

To tell you the truth, all those protests and campaigning were, to say the least, hypocritical. We were young people who wanted to fight for just causes, and that one was another good opportunity for a fight. Our struggle was for our freedom to choose, rather than for the rights of the rats. We did not want to have on our coats the same blood that our student colleagues had. We were boot–biologists, not whitecoat–biologists, and we wanted to detach ourselves from such an unromantic breed. We wanted a bloodless diploma, so we could continue taking samples and collecting creatures with dignity.

We, the boot–scientists, spent a few centuries hunting and collecting live specimens to be able to label them, so we can study them, so we can understand them, and so we can protect them; but when they have all been labelled, there will not be any left to study, understand or protect. We got it all wrong, and we know it. Still, we keep it wrong, because we are convinced we cannot do better. We keep the system as it is, and hope we can find somebody that can pay us for doing it. Our hands are as dirty as everybody else's.

I suppose the bloody ritual worked on me because since then, on more than one occasion I have forgotten the means by being obsessed with the goals. I suppose, after all, they did train me well.

By the way, she did not have a name—I made it up while I was writing. Lab rats do not have names; rule number one.

I stayed with my head down in the weird room for quite some time. I did not dare to look at anyone; I did not dare to look at her. I stood up, and I left.

Chapter Ten
December 19th 2001

The clouds have thickened and this morning is dark. I'd better stay put; I do not want to discover that up here rain clouds do not look like the ones I am used to. Besides, yesterday was a very long session, and I have a lot to write—and a lot to think as well.

There were so many of them, all in the same corner, all avoiding eye contact with me, but perfectly attentive of each of my movements, as always. Many people would find it quite difficult to identify each of them, due to their dark faces and grey coats, as well as the poor lighting conditions of the room. Not in my case, though; I knew them quite well, and because my memory was back I could tell them apart even under those circumstances; Django, Laura, Figu, Tess, Polly, Harry, Hannah, Marvin, Sophie, Tom, Jamie, Flynn, Oscar, George, Freya, and Chico. Who should I pick? One of you? All of you? Then I *eolked*.

At the primate sanctuary where I worked for a few

years we had developed a vocabulary that only people working there would understand. It was not only the fact that the keepers lived on site with the monkeys, so the Sanctuary in itself was a small universe with very precise procedures and terms to describe them (routine, shutting off, monkey cake, do the gym, etc); it was also the fact that we tried to communicate with the monkeys using their language, not ours. This is how the verb 'to eolk' was coined, which means to produce the contact call of the Amazonian Woolly Monkey.

When I *eolked* in the weird room all the woolly monkeys replied but one. Tess said nothing, and she resumed grooming her prehensile tail as if she had not heard a thing.

I met Tess when she was already an adult female, mother of Freya. They were two 'special' females for one particular reason; they did not normally go out from the enclosures into the gardens with the keepers, as the other females did. At that time — not any more — some monkeys would go into the gardens on the days when the sanctuary was opened to the public. This activity — which visitors loved — was only possible with adult females and babies, since adult males are quite dangerous and could attack either visitors or us. Tess and Freya did not like visitors; they always felt very nervous in the gardens, so the decision not to allow them there had been taken well before I joined the team.

In fact, I met Tess the very first day I visited the Sanctuary as a tourist. I was hitch hiking through the British Isles looking for a place to work, and I had already gone through most of Scotland, Ireland, Wales and the North of England. I was doing the South now, and this led me to Cornwall. The driver of one of the lifts mentioned a monkey sanctuary on the south Cornish coast, so it seemed a good idea to pay a visit, and to explore the possibility they would need a zoologist such as me.

I did go, and I fell immediately in love with the place. A Victorian house with big beautiful gardens that go right down to the sea, and a community of lovely keepers that were living together looking after a colony of twenty–odd grey woolly monkeys—extremely close to my idea of paradise.

One of the keepers was 'doing the gym' (one of the interconnected enclosures was called the gym, and a keeper normally stood by it explaining what was going on with the monkeys inside) and he was explaining things about two monkeys that were 'grooming' the grass for insects. The keeper was explaining how one of the monkeys could be recognised because, in an accident when she was a baby, she had lost the tip of her tail. That monkey was Tess.

After a bit of chatting with the keeper I realised they accepted volunteers to help out. Months later I was back volunteering, then becoming a keeper, then the research co–ordinator, then the rehabilitation co–ordinator, and eventually becoming a senior member of staff sharing the directorship of the Sanctuary; five years altogether.

The life at the Sanctuary was quite unusual. The keepers owned the place and ran it as a co–operative, taking all decisions by unanimity in weekly meetings. The monkeys lived in ten interconnected enclosures, mostly outdoors, and the relationship with the keepers was quite personal. The Sanctuary's philosophy was focused on the individual, and the level of care the monkeys received was the best I had seen with captive wild animals so far. Nevertheless, there were problems too, mainly linked to the fact that people lived and worked together for long time, and also to a slightly simplistic approach to things that sometimes created, in my opinion, a disconnection with the real world.

So, I had met Tess from the very beginning. I was always particularly sympathetic with her dislike for visitors—I have to say, I did not like them either. I always had a problem with the part of the keeper's job that involved taking the monkeys out and accompanying them—both as a kind of helper and as a bodyguard—all over the garden—which was often plagued by tourists. I did not mind talking to visitors or giving formal talks—I was well known for my over-enthusiastic forty minutes' talk that had to last only twenty minutes—but I certainly had a problem with accompanying the monkeys out. Therefore, after thirty-odd years of Sanctuary history, I believe I was the first senior keeper that did not take them to the gardens; that I shared with Tess and Freya.

I liked Tess; she seemed to be quite socially skilful because she could avoid creating disruptions, or being in the way of somebody else's problems. She had managed to avoid the bottom of the hierarchy by keeping a low profile but showing confidence when needed. She was quite a good mother too—in fact Freya was learning her mother's ways, and because of that she was not coming out either. What I liked the most, though, is the fact that she seemed to have an existence slightly more disconnected from human keepers than the other monkeys. I always thought that Tess was one of the most real woolly monkeys at the Sanctuary, if you know what I mean.

My duties were gradually shifting away from normal keeper jobs towards one of the Sanctuary's dreams; to rehabilitate the entire colony back to the Amazon, their natural habitat. Since its creation, the Sanctuary had an attitude that could be considered anti–traditional–zoo, and there was the clear recognition that these monkeys should not be living in captivity in Cornwall — the first generation had been rescued pets. My scientific approach, and my facility for learning to speak Portuguese, pushed me deeper and deeper into the rehabilitation project — so much that at times I even considered it my project — which explains my frequent trips to Brazil.

I learnt everything about woolly monkey keeping from the senior keepers, who in turn learnt from other senior keepers, and so on; therefore, after a few years, I became a senior keeper myself, with all the responsibility this entailed.

After spending so much time in Brazil, working at the Sanctuary felt different every time I returned from a trip. I had witnessed many other monkeys of many other species suffer the wrongs of the illegal pet trade and unjustified captivity, and sometimes I felt frustrated at my failure to draw the Sanctuary keepers' attention towards those other monkeys. There was so much to do, and such a long way to go before the Cornish monkeys could be returned back to the Amazon, that I sometimes felt angry at the apparent lack of interest and the air of complacency I could see in the Cornish paradise lifestyle.

It was during these critical times when something very serious was happening in the colony. Although births and deaths had always been common events in the sanctuary life, this time too many health problems were occurring too quickly. Polly, one of the healthiest females, began getting thinner and thinner, and eventually died. Chico, an amazing male who had managed to grow up to adulthood despite the fact he was paraplegic due to a bite in his spine when he was a baby, suddenly died. Not long before, Jamie, a very handsome young male whom everybody had their money on — including me — to be the next leader, collapsed one morning without warning and a few hours later he was dead; the list goes on and on.

During my last couple of years at the Sanctuary half the colony had died, most from causes still unknown; each monkey in its own personal drama, each in its own personal agony. But there is a death I remember particularly well; Tess'.

Tess miscarried her new baby a couple of days after Chico's death, so I was keeping an eye on her while I was doing the gym. My mind was trying to put pieces together to see whether I could figure out what was going on. We had no useful information from any *post mortem*, so we had to guess it all. For me, it was obvious that it was some sort of epidemic, and therefore I thought that it was imperative that we should apply anti cross–contamination procedures, and possibly close to the public for a while. Unfortunately, other keepers did not share my views on the matter, and I felt quite angry about it. While I was having all these thoughts I was continually interrupted by visitor's questions—which did not help.

Between thoughts, explanations, and a lot of pacing, I perceived that Tess' behaviour was changing. She began looking down, and her movements were not quite right. Soon after she found her way from the gym to one of the indoor rooms, room two. Minutes later another keeper and I witnessed her collapsing. We went into the room and tried emergency resuscitation, but nothing worked.

Tess' death was not my first monkey death; it was not the first time I had to take blood directly from the heart of a recently dead body either. However, I found myself unable to do it properly with her; her death, for some reason, had affected me more than the others, and my hand never stopped shaking.

The next morning, accumulated frustration and anger made me leave the Sanctuary for a few days in order to find someplace where I could cool down. I went walking and walking until I ended up on the moors.

With no planning, my feet led me to Dartmoor Prison (an old jail initially used for the American War of the Independence prisoners, but still functioning today). A profound sense of oppression invaded me when I found myself looking at the prison walls. Tall, grey, miles away from civilisation, those walls seemed to have imbedded in them all the tears and sorrows of thousands of captive souls. How utterly wasteful a whole life in captivity had to be behind those walls; how deeply sombre had to be dying by them; and this was a human prison. The monkeys at the Sanctuary had been put in their own private jail not for what they had done, but for who they were. How worse captivity can become, when you are innocent and die in it?

I came back to the Sanctuary and I continued fighting for the return of the remaining monkeys to the Amazon; but disease destroyed the dream. The project was abandoned, with my own direct recommendation, when a new virus was discovered in the group. No, it was not the one that killed Chico, Jamie, Tess and her baby, nor the one that soon after killed Sophie, Tom and Figu; it was a new one that probably has not killed anyone yet, but it may at any time. After five generations in captivity, despite all possible good care and dedication, nature could not be forced any more.

What is the moral of this story? That captivity is bad, and no matter how much you do to help a captive animal, it always will hate you for that? Come on, this is too simple. Why was Tess the only one who did not respond to my *eolk* in the weird room, then?

OK, I was an animal keeper, and therefore responsible for keeping the animals alive and well. I failed, they suffered, and they died. But I fought for their wellbeing, and I even fought to take them back to where they belonged. I did it against all odds, and against people's attitudes, and with all available knowledge and tools I had at that moment. How much more can a keeper do?

OK, I was also a zoo director. I shared the directorship with many others, and it was not a conventional zoo whatsoever — more of an anti–zoo centre, in fact — but it did keep exotic animals in captivity and displayed them to the public, and therefore it was a zoo. In all fairness, I was partially responsible for the policy of the Sanctuary, and its actions as an institution. Did we not try to close ourselves down by returning all the animals to their natural habitat? Did we not operate in an un–zoo–like way in which the individual animals' interests counted much more than the visitors' or the staff's? Did we not promote a world without zoos by educating the public about the ethics of captivity?

OK, I was a primate rehabilitator, and I quit my job without having achieved any successful rehabilitation of any animal back to its natural habitat. Furthermore, in the end, once the new virus was discovered, I was instrumental in preventing the Cornish monkeys returning to the Amazon. But I reacted in a responsible manner preventing the possible disaster of a failed rehabilitation attempt, and even worse, the possible introduction of a new pathogen into the wild. Yes, the breeding, I know. If the Sanctuary had prevented breeding from the start many monkeys would have avoided suffering; many lives would not have been wasted. This is true, but I am not to blame for the breeding policy established before I worked at the Sanctuary, only for the breeding while I was a senior member of the staff there, and in that time there was plenty of justification. The chances to survive in Brazil once rehabilitated would have increased with a well establish multi–aged social group, in which youngsters would play a very important role in learning about the new life. Once the rehabilitation plan was cancelled the breeding stopped, and I contributed to that decision too.

I accept my responsibilities as keeper, zoo director and rehabilitator, and I accept also my failures during all these three roles, but such failures did not come from having made the wrong moral decision, but for ineptitude, misfortune, and especially for trying to achieve the impossible. I cannot be blamed for that. I felt for them, I felt their suffering! My walk to the prison must prove that!

One of the monkeys in the weird room moved out from the corner it was sitting and approached me. He was Django, the oldest monkey of the group. I was a bit uneasy with that because he was an adult male known for grabbing distracted keepers through the wire (we had a quasi–non–contact policy with adult males, due to their aggressiveness and strength), so I was not used to seeing him in the same room as me. He sat on my lap and, in an obvious posture for requesting grooming, he then extended his arm back.

Django was the only monkey left from the second generation of monkeys at the Sanctuary — his parents, therefore, had been born in the wild. He lived 25 years at Cornwall but never became the leader of the group — his nephew, Charlie, beat him on that. For the keepers Django was something else. He had some privileges other monkeys did not have; not due to favouritism, but because of respect. Django had been there long before the most experienced keeper had joined the team, and he knew the Sanctuary through all its evolution, from the almost circus–like shows in the 1960s, to the rehabilitation dreams in the 1990s. He was also the monkey that sooner or later would appear in a keeper's dreams. There was something mystical in Django; he had a profound impact on everybody, and I was not an exception.

I was touched when Django sat on my lap for a groom in the weird room. As if I had been forgiven for my sins, as if he recognised I had done my best; but when I went to groom him he suddenly grabbed my jacket and began shaking me vigorously. The other monkeys stood on all fours and began producing a rhythmic vocalisation known as a 'worrying call'.

I did not know what to do; I was aware that in normal circumstances all those woollies attacking me would have been my end, but these were hardly normal circumstances. I put my hand on my mouth and I produced sobbing noises, as a woolly monkey would do trying to befriend another under a tense situation — keepers used this occasionally. Django stopped the shaking and joined me in the ritualised behaviour. A few seconds later all the other monkeys moved towards us, stopped their worrying calls and, producing very high pitched squeaks, joined us in a big hugging/sobbing session.

When we were calmed they all scattered over the room; Django sat a couple of feet from me. I still had my hand on my mouth, I was crouched over my knees and I was looking at them over my glasses not quite knowing what to do next. I gradually recovered a normal posture; I was glad that I had not forgotten the basic rules of woolly monkey etiquette.

Why had Django attacked me? Why had he come,

offered his arm to me, and then attacked me?

Well, he did not attack me, really. He did not bite or anything; he only shook me a little bit. That's right, he shook me, as an adult would do either as a telling off or as a status display. Was he telling me off for all my failures while working at the Sanctuary? Was he a witness for the prosecution?

No, he was not doing it for me, but he was doing it for the others. He did it for the sobbing session; he used me as a way to get the group together. He is the leader now; he has made himself the leader and, after all this time, he decided to go for it. I was not even a part of it; I was just a human, a human to out–rank.

Tess lived and died within the walls of her prison, and yet she chose not to go out into the gardens in order to stay away from people. No, Tess did not respond to my *eolk* because I failed her more than I failed all the others. She did not respond because she does not like visitors, and I, after all, was just another visitor; one that stayed longer, that's all.

Who are worse, the merciless poachers, the unscrupulous dealers, the heartless breeders, the greedy sellers, the irresponsible owners, the patronising rescuers, the disrespectful visitors or the naïve rehabilitators? The worst are the ones that pay for all the above and think of themselves as the saviours. The worst are the ones that say they feel the animal's suffering, because they cannot. The worst are the hypocrites.

I am guilty not just for what I did, but also for who I am; another pretentious human being.

Chapter Eleven
December 20th 2001

I can see the clouds moving fast; first from North to South, and now from West to East. There is no wind down here, but up there in the sky things must be quite different. I can perceive a distinct line in the clouds that makes me think that a front is approaching; whether it is a cold or a warm front, I do not know, but it does carry thicker clouds with it. I guess that we will soon find out.

Yesterday I cooked a big pot of rice, potatoes and cabbage; I almost burnt it, but I saved it just in time. It is going to last me for ages, but it is not going to replace noodles as my main staple food — well, also porridge in the morning, of course. Years ago I used to cook much more; I liked to experiment with new combinations and exotic ingredients, but nowadays I have succumbed to the empire of the Microwave — everything falls in 'time', doesn't it?

Up here time is also important, believe it or not. With the short days — and every day getting shorter — and my evening trial I am under pressure to write fast. I do not know whether I will be able to cope with this rhythm. It does help that it is warmer now than the initial days—it is difficult to hit the right key when you are shaking.

It's funny how sometimes fantasy imposes its right to exist. On some occasions, when I was zoo checking around the country, people I met asked me about what I was doing. Since I did not know if the person talking to me was a friend or a relation of the local zoo owner I was investigating, I had to be careful about what I said. Most of the time I said I was a Spanish tourist, but sometimes this cover did not work. When people realised that I was only after zoological collections, or when they saw I spent afternoons and evenings shut in my B&B room—writing a report of the day's visit—I needed another cover story. On those occasions I normally said that I was writing a book about animals; it is funny how it turned out to be true, after all.

I am a bit worried, though, about how the trial is going. Although I can always defend myself it seems that in the end I am the one that accuses myself. In fact, nobody has ever accused me. I do not know where this is going. Has everything I have done been wrong? Would any justification I use be insufficient? Am I supposed to change something in my life as a consequence of the sessions, or should I just forget about it? What sort of sentence am I going to get?

I think I have been taking the trial too frivolously, as if I could detach from it every morning, as if it were some sort of show I am watching on TV, on the TV in my head. Yesterday, for instance, it was almost as if I was watching a soap opera.

I am still unsure whether I am the one who picks the next animal in the weird room or the animals pick me, but in yesterday's session it was clearly their choice. I was looking at Mico Tião, the chimp from Rio Zoo, when a noise behind my neck began bothering me. It was some sort of flying insect; at first I thought that it was just a fly — after all, with the room full of animals flies would be predictable uninvited guests — but soon I recognised that distinctive vibrato — like the noise bicycles produce when they go very fast down hill and the pedals are not being used.

Surely enough, the insect landed on the back of my left hand. I took my glasses off — I have to do that these days when I want to look very close at something — and I recognised the marking on the thorax; one green enamel dot on the top left hand corner, and another one on the middle. Yes, it is she; it is V5, the most amazing wasp that ever lived.

I was in my second year at the University when I had to write a dissertation for the General Zoology class. Because I intended to get a good mark for it — I was a vocational zoologist, and I wanted this to be reflected in my grade — I decided that apart from doing the usual bibliographic work I should do some fieldwork too. I just needed an animal I could study easily without having to go too far, but that was also slightly unusual and interesting enough. Around that time I was attending some extra curricular lessons in Ethology (the discipline that studies animal behaviour) given by a lecturer well known for his challenging views and grabbing talks — who later became my mentor — so I thought I might ask him for advice. He suggested I could do my dissertation on social wasps, and he knew a place not far from the faculty with an available active nest.

Wasps were the ideal subjects; everybody hates them, dangerous to work with, complex social behaviour, and common everywhere. I took my notebook and I went to the old brick structure where the nest was. It was some sort of ventilation shaft, about two metres tall, placed in the middle of an empty field that was often used as an improvised parking site when a big football match was on. The first few days not much happened; wasps coming in and out, apparent random activity, a little bit of apprehension on my part, etc.

One day I built up confidence and I decided to get a little bit closer. I slowly approached the brick hole leading to the entrance of the nest—trying not to move anything too fast so they would not detect me and set the alarm off. Then, something happened that very much changed my life from that point onwards. One of the wasps that was in the entrance suddenly stopped what she was doing and slowly turned her head around to look at me. My heart began pumping faster and faster, but I kept still. The wasp, to my surprise, had a face. It was not like a fly or a bee (with a faceless head), but it had a distinctive face, flat with two long elliptical eyes, and she was looking straight at mine; not at me, not at my body, but straight at my face. I remember that my skin became gooseflesh—it is happening now, as it does any time I remember the event—and my heart went crazy.

That was a little person I was looking at, and she was looking at me and judging whether it was worth raising the alarm, to go and sting me, or to fly away from me. She reflected, and I sweated...and eventually she turned her head around and resumed what she was doing. So powerful was that experience for me that from that moment on I could not rest until I had learnt everything about this tiny people that, in that short event, had shown me the courage, the mercy, and the wisdom I often missed in human beings. From that day on I spent 10 years studying that particular type of wasp, and I earned the deserved nickname of 'the waspman'.

They belong to the genus *Polistes*, which in Greek means 'the people that build cities'. It is a cosmopolitan genus with species all over the world, with the exception of cold countries, New Zealand and, sadly, Britain. *Polistes* are not just social wasps that build paper nests; they are a missing link in the evolution of society; they are one of the first insects that made the step from being solitary to being social. They do not have that organisational level that most ants, bees, termites or other social wasps have, which make them look totally alien to us. No, their societies are simpler, but the individual and its individuality have a role in them. They are, pretty much, in the same social evolutionary stage that we are. They are the closest insects to human beings I have ever seen.

I studied them everywhere I could; in the countryside, in the city, by the sea, by the roads, and even at the top of high mountains. I built a one–metre model wasp which I hung in my living room to get my senses used to their aposematic colours (combinations of red and black, red and blue, etc) that makes us (mammals) instinctively uncomfortable in their presence. I learnt to get closer to them without creating any disturbance, so I could look deep inside their everyday activities. I learnt how to avoid being stung, and I understood their reasons for doing it. I spent countless hours photographing and video– recording them at night while I had to work during the day to survive. I kept studying them even when I was penniless, years after my degree had finished, and I could not find anyone that would finance my PhD — they do not produce honey, and everybody hates wasps, remember? I became so obsessed, that when I had the chance to study bonobos (pygmy chimps) instead, and maybe escape from my economic and academic cul–de–sac, I decided to continue with my wasps.

After my first five years of studying wasps I had an important breakthrough. Up until then, to figure out what the complex social interactions between individual wasps meant, I had to rely on either slow–motion video viewing, or indirect deduction. They move too fast and everything happens very quickly in the wasp world; after all, they only have a year to live their whole life. After five years focusing on their tiny bodies and tuning my time perception to theirs, one day, out of the blue, I understood without any aid a complete social interaction while it was happening. Finally, despite all the sceptics' advice, I had managed to empathise with an insect, as a primatologist can do with an ape. Since then, I reached the level that pretty much meant I could just watch and learn.

It was during this empathic phase that I met V5. She was the queen of the nest I was studying at home at that time. Her name came from the code of painted enamel I had to use to recognise each individual — V stands for 'verd', which is the Catalan for 'green', and 5 was the number assigned to a particular combination of painted dots on the wasp's thorax.

Polistes queens are not like other social insect queens. They should be called Presidents, I think, because one of the wonders of the *Polistes* world is that, given the circumstances, even a very low ranking worker can became the queen of the colony—which is particularly remarkable because workers are sterile, but they can become fertile if pushed towards a more 'political' role. This amazing peculiarity makes *Polistes'* society very flexible and dynamic, so once you are able to see what is going on, it is sometimes like watching a soap opera — or even better, a miniature Hamlet.

There was a particular aspect I wanted to study. I had already seen how a colony that lost its queen—by a hungry bird, for example—continued with a substitute taking over the crown, but I always wondered whether all the other wasps would ever remember the old queen—especially if the new one turned out to be 'difficult'. Conventional wisdom would say that no memory of the old queen would be kept whatsoever; but then again, *Polistes* are not conventional wasps. So, I set up an experiment in order to find out.

One morning, when everybody was still sleeping in the colony, I took V5 out (that was the equivalent of a bird having eaten the queen). No, I did not kill her, I kept her alive and well in a separate compartment, where I regularly provided her with everything she needed. Surely enough, the colony, when they discovered they were queenless, began re–organising themselves and finally a new queen took over; V1. That was a particularly predictable event, since V1 and V5 had been long time rivals. V1 was in fact older than V5, but somehow lost some crucial fights with her younger sister in key moments of the colony development, so she had remained in a very close second position — she was what is known as the 'beta' female.

I left the colony stabilising itself during what in human time would be an equivalent of several decades. After that I decided to free the old queen and allow her to return to the nest (that would be the equivalent of a queen having being taken away in a storm, for example, and then managing to return to the nest using its amazing homing abilities). What happened next was truly incredible.

V5 flew straight to the nest, and when she landed there the guards on duty immediately threw her out — they were new wasps that had been born after she left. V5 tried again, but by then the entire colony had already been alerted. Then, a micro–event happened — which I would have missed if I had tried the experiment years earlier. Some of the wasps she knew went to join the guards in throwing her away, but for a split of a second, they hesitated. Immediately, V1 — angrier than I had ever seen her — appeared from behind and dived into V5 with all the power a wasp can deliver. Others joined the attack, and V5 escaped, lucky to not have been stung.

That would have been the end of the experiment apart from the fact that the wasp involved was, as I said, the most extraordinary wasp that ever lived. V5 did not give up, and every day tried again and again — she knew the score, and she knew that V1 could not be vigilant all the time. V5 tried, on several occasions, to interact with wasps of her old nest when they were flying away from it. They seemed to recognise her then, and she was not attacked outside the nest.

One day there was an emergency in the nest. The temperature had risen too much and it was threatening the development of the larvae. On such occasions the 'fire' alarm is given, and wasps start to ventilate (moving their wings and holding onto the nest with their legs, in order to create a current of colder air). If this does not do the job, some scouts would go out to get some water which would be sprayed on the nest to cool it down — yes, this is what they are doing by the water on summer days before you start panicking and try to hit them. We had a cooling emergency in our nest, and most wasps were ventilating. Then, seeing the opportunity, V5 flew to the nest and started ventilating with the others. You could see that V1 did not like that at all, but she could not do anything; the larvae wellbeing is paramount. At last V5 managed to stay in the nest, but holding the lowest possible hierarchical position; male wasp.

I have not told you about males yet. In *Polistes* terms males are considered social parasites. They do not contribute to the colony work, and often they are kicked out first thing in the morning. As a result they fly around in bachelor groups, drinking nectar and having fights — I swear to you, I am not lost in an anthropomorphic delusion. In the evening, though, they are allowed to return home, and next morning kicked out again. There is only one thing that males do for the group; ventilate in an overheating emergency. So, V5 was allowed to stay, as long as she stayed as a low ranking male–like worker.

V5, who was once the queen of the colony, was not content with it. Day after day she fought with others, helped out, made friends with the ones she knew, and step by step she climbed higher and higher in the hierarchy, always staying away from V1 and her knights. Eventually she had been re–accepted by most wasps, and she only needed to face the most dominant.

One morning it happened. I dropped off watching the nest—days and nights of neglecting myself, totally absorbed by the drama—and suddenly I was awoken by a terrible fight. I could not see who was involved; it was too quick, too intense. I looked around for all the other wasps; V7, R3, R8...I could not find V5...or V1; they had to be the ones that were fighting. The fight took ages in wasp time, but finally one of the wasps made a few steps back, and bowed down keeping all her body touching the nest surface; that wasp was V1. Exhausted, V5 approached the now submissive rival and put her leg on top of V1's thorax—this is the ritualised gesture that confirms dominance in the *Polistes* language. Soon after, each and every one of the colony wasps offered their submission to V5, who touched them all in similar fashion. V5, after a lifetime of struggle, was again the queen of the colony; and when the last wasp had paid her respects, V5 died there, on the spot.

I took her out and I did everything I could imagine to bring her back to life; cleaning her spiracles with a brush, feeding honey directly to her mouth, even—naively—using some batteries to pass an electrical current through her body. The old queen V5 had died.

In the weird room V5 was now back, on my left hand. I wondered whether she was going to sting me. I would deserve it, because I was the dragon that kidnapped her; I was the monster that made her lose her kingdom, and eventually her life; I was the god that nourished her misfortune.

I was brought up as Catholic but I soon abandoned religion, before my teens. I did not substitute it with any pseudo–religious belief or anything like that; I just grew out of it, as much as a Catholic can — there is always some residual imagery left in an ex–Catholic brain, though. Nevertheless, I cannot say that I lack spirituality. Nature has always been my temple; if something made me think that there was something more than me and my human world, that was always a natural phenomenon, never a supernatural one. If Nature goes, if we get rid of it, then we will understand what it really means to be alone; that is when we will truly feel like orphans.

I suppose that for a long time I have not seen the world as if somebody is up there watching us; and yet, I was the one who watched over the wasp world, and made terrible things happen to it. Can we blame God for our misfortunes as V5 can blame me? Can we blame God for our mistakes? Or Gaia, or the Cosmic Order of Things?

If any form of God exists, animals could believe in Him as much as we do. If He does not exist, animals could still believe in Him, as we do. Why are we then so sure that we are the only ones that can believe in something that does not depend on logic, but on faith? Was not logic an attribute we used to think animals did not possess? It is a disturbing thought to imagine animals praying to God when they wait for slaughter, is it not?

In terms of spirituality it is not the existence or not of God, or the following of a particular religion instead of another, which matters. What really matters is the individual's feeling of something beyond its reach, its comprehension, its domain. Nobody is in control of everything, nor has absolute knowledge, and therefore everybody can have spiritual feelings, even a wasp. I felt them when I saw the first *Polistes* looking at me, showing me that there was a world I had no access to. Then, obsessed as mad, I created my little personal religion in order to seek that truth I had the chance to glimpse at only for a moment.

In moral judgement it is not the world beyond the clouds that matters, but the world we can control, the world we can affect, the world we live in, not on; the options we could have chosen, the effects we could have predicted, the outcomes we could have avoided and the actions we can regret.

V5 eventually flew away off my hand. Because she did not blame me, she did not sting me. She could have done it, she was perfectly capable of feeling bitterness and judging others. She could have done it because she was totally able to see me as an entity worth stinging. She did not blame me because my actions were beyond her reach, beyond the scope of her moral judgement. She never lived a day without my face hovering in her world. I was her god, the one that pulled the strings of her universe without telling why, and she did not blame me for that; but I can blame myself for what I did to her. I did it to satisfy my thirst for knowledge; to be able to cross into the wasp's world, and have my own spiritual experience fulfilled. I can blame myself because I did it just for me, for my own personal satisfaction. We cannot blame God for our mistakes; but He can.

Chapter Twelve
December 21st 2001

I was awoken in the middle of the night by a metallic sound; rain was falling on the cottage roof. At first only in small amounts, as if a few small isolated clouds had passed by, but later it became more intense and durable; it has been raining since. It is not a very loud noise but it is impossible to ignore up here. In fact, I almost couldn't sleep after the first drops fell.

It is quite dark outside—and quite warm also, I should say; I suppose it is normal. I am worried the cottage may have a black out this evening because of the rain; I have been putting candles all over the place, so I will be prepared if it happens; I always carry a small torch in my pocket, just in case.

Today I do not feel like chatting. I'll get straight to it.

I had not seen her in the weird room before, and I had wondered why she was not there with all the others. It had to mean something special, but I could not figure out what. Surely I was accountable for her suffering and her death.

Why had she not come? Why was she not part of it?

Yesterday, though, she was there. I felt her presence right from the moment I entered the room; I felt her wisdom, her warmth, and her integrity. I do not think I ever got closer to any animal than I was to her. She taught me many things, important lessons that I have used on many occasions. She was the family pet for a long time, but she was not my pet at all; she was my friend; she had been, for a long while, my only friend.

We called her Nit — which means 'night' in Catalan — because she was a black puppy when she was born, but when she grew up her colour changed to the traditional black and blonde of the pure–breed Alsatians.

Things at home were quite different now. We had a brand new democracy, and Catalan culture was, at last, allowed to flourish freely without restraints. There was an effervescence of political parties — many illegal when the General was still alive — and now children on the street collected party stickers rather than rubber bullets. The 'grey people' had long gone — although they had only changed the colour of their uniform — and 'transition' was the favourite word. The economy was growing fast, and so was the city, with American burger restaurants opening everywhere and old slum areas being redeveloped — including the gypsy area behind my house. Those were exciting times because we felt very European, kiosks displayed things we had all dreamt about and, of course, 'the force' was with everybody.

I, on the other hand, was trapped in an 'adolescence' black hole, which seemed to extend itself well beyond what I had anticipated. The older I was getting, the more I realised how different were the ones I had thought equal, and how equal were the ones I had thought different. I did not understand people, but I felt very close to animals. Was that a sign of de–humanisation, or just the opposite? Why had one to be a philanthropist when one could care for more than humans? Why care about people when you could care about every living thing, including people? It seemed that the world had chosen to buy a single ticket, when the return ticket cost the same. I decided to buy my own ticket, and to travel alone.

My personal universes gained momentum every day and my social integration lost priority. Old friends found new friends and I did not try to replace them, but despite the strength of my cocoon my need to communicate with others managed to pop out every now and then; I found myself talking to my lamp (Carmen), my telescope (Felip) and, of course, Nit.

I used to talk long to Nit about the things that bothered me and, although I knew perfectly well that she was not able to understand me, her patience did comfort me. After all, she was much cheaper than any therapist, and nicer to hug.

My conversations with Nit developed some sort of mutual understanding that went to surprising limits. Sometimes it was Nit that came to me as if asking me for a chat. Sometimes I seemed to understand her problems, and I talked to her about them as if we were reversing roles. Soon a strong bond was created that surprised most of my family. Without me even noticing it, my behaviour with her became less and less human; spending a long time with her on the floor, stopping giving her orders (talking as a 'master'), etc. In fact, when my parents wanted her to do something she seemed reluctant to do, they asked me to persuade her, because they knew she would do it if I talked to her. We often ended up sleeping on top of each other under the table, as if we were a couple of puppies.

It was through this relationship that I began understanding what being a pet is like. I could not help but feel empathy when family friends came to visit and my parents asked her to perform some tricks; they had asked me a few years earlier and I did mine as well as she did hers. I also understood her devotion to my father, the pack leader, and her loyalty to all the members of my family. I did not see love there, I saw duty. She would do anything to please my father, and the thought of failing him terrified her. You could see her jumping about and wagging her tail when he came home, but also her ears were back and her lips were retracted—there was a conflict there, that was not joy. She was a pack animal, the pack meant everything to her survival, and the leader meant everything to the pack.

I then realised how much her life depended on her skills to perform the social role of family pet well. We still lived in that flat with the small balcony, and she also had to go on the lead when we took her for a walk. She always wanted to go out, and had to beg for it; and if she wanted to run, we had to be in the mood to run with her. She totally depended on us for food—she had been condemned to be permanently at the bottom of the pack hierarchy, so she had to wait for the hunting group to come back and 'regurgitate' the catch of the day. She had no choice other than to be nice and hope that food would come soon. If she did something wrong she would be punished; if we wanted to go somewhere she would be left at home waiting; if she wanted to follow that scent she had to be patient; if she wanted that biscuit she had to sit...

I kept finding parallels in her 'profession' as family pet and mine as family boy; her eyes showed me that she was suffering her profession as much as I was suffering mine.

Time passed by, and although we were both growing up, she was doing it faster than I was. By the time I was in my late teens, she was a mature lady, and she knew things about life that I could never imagine (even after having spent her whole life in that small flat). She knew anything there was to know about human social behaviour, and she taught me how to deal with it. Guided by her as if I was blind I crawled out of my black hole and became socially normal — well, almost.

She was a pure–breed Alsatian, with the right ears, the right colour, the right behaviour, but also the right genetic diseases. Her genes made her develop progressive arthrosis in the rear limbs, which made her suffer a lot of pain when walking. She was, nevertheless, as eager to go downstairs for a walk as ever, to join the pack in any hunting that was planned. Later on, parasitic protozoa caught up with her, and she lost her hair, her mobility and her spark. Still, she kept performing her role well, while privately dreaming of an alternative life as a wolf.

I could no longer allow her life to continue like that.

She had helped me during my troubles, she had taught me how to be human, she had always been loyal to me and to the rest of the pack, and she had kept her tears well hidden inside. Now, it was time for my last lesson. She had to teach me how to die.

I took her in my arms and I told her I was going to kill her. I told her that her pain would be gone soon, and that her duties would no longer be necessary. I told her that she had to leave the pack because her body was too old. I told her that I was sorry for her life and for everything we had done to her.

In my arms she fought, and she fought up to the last second, but while she was going I looked into her eyes and realised that she was fighting for me, not for her; to teach me another lesson, the last one, the most important. To teach me about holding on to life, no matter how miserable it can be, how lonely, how hard.

She was born as a pet, she lived as a pet, and she died as a pet. But she was not. She was a lost lonely wolf.

I was dying to go and hug her in the weird room, but I did not do it. With her I was not a human who could do what I wanted when I wanted to. With her, I was a member of her pack, and by now she had risen high in the pecking order. I wanted to jump and wag my tail, but I had none. Nervously smiling, I looked at her, with tears in my eyes, waiting for some signal.

I did kill her, with my own hands, but that was not murder. She would have fought more, she wouldn't have given up, and she wouldn't have died if I had not done it. Yes, I did it against her will, but I did it for her; she could not walk, she could not bark, she could not eat. No, that was not murder, no matter what you think; that was most definitely not murder. She was my friend, and you do not murder your friend.

But this is not it, is it? This is not why she is here; it is not her death but her life, is it?

There is something behind our pets' love we do not want to see and that we do not want to talk about; fear, fear of you, fear of others, fear of being alone, fear of being abandoned. It terrifies us not just because it explains our pets' behaviour better than love does, but also because it is the fundamental force that makes us keep a pet in the first place. We want to touch people we like, but we fear their reaction; we want to feel wanted by people, but we fear they will want somebody else; we want to look after others, but we fear others want to look after themselves; we want something warm to hold, but we fear everything around us may be cold. We get our pets because of fear. We do love them, we need to love them, and we love to need them.

Pets' fear is much more justifiable than ours is. We have made them so dependent on us that most of the time they would truly be in trouble without us. 'We give them anything they need', we think. 'You may not give me what I need', they think. 'Sit down, and I'll give you your dinner', we say. 'I will sit down, or you won't be giving me any dinner', they think. 'Look how happy you are to see me', we think; 'I thought you never would return', they think. And yet, how many pets have been imprinted with such fear, and then abandoned by their owners when they did not do the pet job well enough?

It is not just that. We not only want them totally dependent on us, but we want them to look totally dependent on us. We change their size, their colour, their ears, their weight, their limbs, their behaviour, and everything we can change until their dependence is so absolute that it even shows up when they sleep. We do not care whether they die of the diseases those new shapes and colours carry with them; they have to die of something anyway.

What about the other pets, the ones we do not hold, the ones we do not pat? Why people think that a goldfish in a tank in somebody's living room is in a better situation than an abused lion in a bad zoo? For that fish the existence or not of the lion does not make any difference to its suffering. The pain in somebody's finger is not better than the pain of a third degree burns patient victim of a fire accident. Both deserved to be cured; both cry with the same tears. All pain should be treated, because pain matters to the individual, and for those individuals other individuals' pain does not alleviate theirs. This is why the captive goldfish ends up losing its mind as the captive lion does; they only know their own ghosts.

The moment we begin deciding who is in pain and who is not, who deserves care and who does not, who matters and who does not, we will end up with the ultimate selfishness; we, only we matter. These are the bases of racism, xenophobia, classism, oligarchy, corruption, sexism, fascism, bigotry and all politically correct forms of evil.

If only pet lovers loved animals more than pets, they could read their eyes better than their tails, and learn something.

Who do I think I am to write such a patronising statement? How much did I learn from Nit that made me immune to criticism?

I learnt to be social, to fight for life, to keep my feelings and to survive; but I did not learn how to respect, or how to stop an animal becoming a pet, or how to stop a pet becoming a toy. I just went along with everything, and when reality was so unbearable that I could not face it anymore I got rid of it, as everyone else does.

No, there is not a drop of redemption in my blood. How many times was I watching TV when I could have taken her out for a walk? How many times did I shout at her to shut up when she was just defending our territory? How many times did I tell her off when she could not wait for us to arrive and open the balcony? How many times did I allow her to go along with the solicited tricks? How many times did I pull her neck when I wanted to go right rather than left? How many, how many times did I say that she was mine, that she was MY dog! Millions, millions of times! And then I got rid of her; I killed her, I killed her as anyone else kills theirs.

I learnt nothing; I learnt nothing at all.

Chapter Thirteen
December 22nd 2001

Something is wrong; something is very wrong. This morning I was woken up by the usual sound of cowbells when I realised that the sun was not up yet. I tried to sleep a bit longer but for some reason I could not sleep any more. After some time I looked at my watch and I pushed the little button that lights the numbers; it was 8:30 and still completely dark—I knew that the days were getting shorter, but that seemed too big a jump to me.

Well, I am up now, it's half past nine, and it is still pitch black. I do not know what is going on; I went out to see whether I could detect any trace of light but I could not see any, none whatsoever. This is something else; one thing is to spend the evenings with the animals from my memory, but the other is this. I thought that I had it all figured out; I thought that, due to the lack of stimulation, I was projecting into my conscience all the guilt I have been accumulating over the years. I thought that it was some sort of auto–cleansing; some time in the wilderness to clear out my veins of caffeine, my muscles of fat, and my brain of guilt. This is something else.

Should I go to the weird room? Should I go now, or wait for later? I don't like this; something is wrong; I don't know what to do.

What choices do I have? I should write what happened yesterday, that's it. I cannot go into the room if I have not written what happened yesterday. I'll do that, I'll write everything and when I finish I'll go back in.

When I entered the weird room there was no room any more; instead, a dark empty hall. I could not see the end of it but I could perceive its size — the sound of the door opening echoed all over. It did not feel cold and the jacket I always take to go to the sessions seemed unnecessary; but I did not take it off.

Yes, this was a completely different scenario; yet, thinking about it, it was no weirder than the animal sessions, so I took the small torch I carry in my pocket and I walked in — leaving the door open behind me. My torch was not very powerful and I could not see much more than the floor in front of me (it was made of shiny stone, like black marble). I could hear no sound, only my own steps and the friction of my clothes. I pointed the torch higher to look at the ceiling but if there was one it was too high to be reached by the weak light.

A faint sound was coming from my left; it was rhythmic and high pitched, but I could not tell what it was yet. I pointed the light in that direction and still I could not see anything. It got louder and louder until I thought I recognised what it was. It was the sound of an animal, an animal walking—galloping in fact—towards me; it was the sound of hooves, small hooves.

A shape arose in the distance; small, pale, round... it was a sheep. I wished I could tell if this was the same sheep that was outside the cottage, or among the rocks, or by the castle, but I could not. It looked like an ordinary sheep to me, as all the others did. When she got closer she began slowing down—the gallop became a walk. When she got to where I was she passed me by. I pointed the torch at her when she was disappearing, but then she stopped and turned her head towards me. I got closer and she resumed walking to her destination.

Looking all around me with the torch I followed her, but I still could not see anything else other than the sheep in front of me. Suddenly, I noticed that the angle of the floor was changing; we were going up hill now, and the more we walked, the steeper the floor felt. Eventually the sheep stopped at what seemed like a flat surface, at the top of the hill. I walked up and stopped by her side.

Faint light began shining from the distance; it looked crepuscular, as if there was a simultaneous sunrise in all directions. After a while I noticed that the hall was bigger than I thought; in fact, as big as it could be. Then I saw something; the silhouettes of millions of figures that were covering the entire floor. When the light became bright enough I could see that they were, of course, animals. Millions and millions of animals; cows, pigs, sheep, birds, in all possible directions, from as far as I could see to the very top of the hill where I was standing. They were all still, quiet and looking in my direction, just like the animals in the weird room the first day. This time, though, there was no monkey, rat, dog or cat, but only pigs, sheep, cattle, poultry...I realised what this session was about.

Growing up in Barcelona I had no idea of what being vegetarian meant. In my school days I had only met one, a very skinny schoolmate who did not seem to enjoy life much, and whose strict parents belonged to a religious pseudo–sect — I thought at first that vegetarianism was some sort of disease. Meat seemed so essential for everything that was culturally important that not eating it as a form of voluntary diet was considered quite preposterous. Also, when times were rough, meat products were the first to go, so if you wanted to bring up a family avoiding any feeling of misery, you would do your best to be sure that meat was always present on the plate. Meat was a given — like being Catholic, having a gender or avoiding pain.

Later on, when I discovered that you could be vegetarian on animal welfare grounds, I thought that it was too late for me; I believed that I was already too addicted to meat and animal products to succeed in any attempt to change my diet. I could not find a way towards vegetarianism that did not bring me back to where I started. I was of the opinion that many vegetarians did not become more involved in animal welfare issues because they already believed that they had made enough 'sacrifice' for the animals' cause. I met many vegetarians that only jumped on the bandwagon for fashion, for religious reasons, for habit, to stop getting fat, or because somebody they liked was on it.

I did not wanted to join the wagon, I thought that the wagon people did not really care about animals, but about themselves, their image, their weight, or their favourite pop singer.

Besides, any of my attempts at becoming vegetarian had failed; I found myself unable to find the line. Which animals can I eat, and which not? Why do some vegetarians eat chicken? Why do some eat fish? Why do some eat eggs? Why do some consume dairy produce? OK, Vegans, that had to be the only consistent way; but what about plants? Are they not alive and then killed to feed Vegans? Macrobiotics, Fruitarians, maybe these were the solution...but where are they? I always ended at the same point I had started at, justifying my omnivourism (i.e. eating everything) by being unable to draw the line, and by making a distinction between eating a dead animal and treating a living one badly. If vegetarians thought that by ordering vegetarian food in a normal restaurant they would prevent the animal being eaten at the next table from suffering a life of frustration and pain, vegetarians were wrong.

If being vegetarian was only a political stand — a good way to make people think about animals and to discuss them during a dinner, for example — then when vegetarianism became mainstream in some circles that aspect was lost. In those circles, which were the circles I tended to be around when I moved to the UK, being omnivorous was exception enough to generate discussions about the topic, and therefore that gave me the chance to point out that animals were still suffering out there.

There was also the argument of indigenous cultures that would have to abandon their balanced omnivorous diet and cut their local forest in order to plant soya beans for the milk substitute of the hypocritical foreigners' breakfast.

In other words, I have always managed to rationalise my omnivourism, and by having a very small amount of meat in my diet, and only choosing the organic option, I could sleep at night.

That was until now; the immense hall full of animals had changed my perspective on the matter. The view of all the animals that had been directly or indirectly fed to me—by me—during my lifetime was something difficult to forget. I realised that if I had been a predator whose life had depended on killing I would probably have had fewer deaths on my shoulders than I had then, and I was supposed to be somebody that respected animals and fought for their rights.

Looking at them, it is easier to see that they have feelings than to see that they are edible; and yet, people question the first and accept the second. I do not question the first, so I have no excuses for accepting the second.

It does not matter whether people do not eat meat for the wrong reasons, in the same way that it does not matter they do not kill others for the wrong reasons either. It does not matter that a theoretical line cannot be drawn. It is not a question of types but a question of individuals. I could have chosen not to eat that lamb, this chicken, that pig...it is not a way of life, a religious belief, or a cultural trend; it is a decision between you and each animal involved; because it is your life, and it is their life too.

I might have been right in not becoming 'a vegetarian', but I was wrong in eating meat. I was wrong in eating them, and not even thinking about who they were.

Chapter Fourteen
December 23rd 2001

I am tired; I want to go to bed, but I cannot. I have to write this; I have to keep writing. As long as I can find a way to the laptop I have to keep coming back to it. That may be my only way out, my only cotton thread in this enchanted land.

It is still dark today. It is dark and windy and the whole house is creaking—I could not sleep properly because of that. I had to go outside with the torch to get to the toilet—I do not want to go through the weird room until I am ready—and I was very cold during the whole process. I am going to light a fire straight away—luckily I still have plenty of wood in the porch.

***

I feel dirty, I have not washed myself for ages, and now that the bathroom is out of reach the only thing I can do is use the kitchen sink. I still have food, including that pot of half–burnt rice that never seems empty.

I have no idea what is going to happen today in the room. I was lucky yesterday when I left the door open and I could find my way out. If I had closed it I might have been lost in there forever. Maybe I should be prepared today; I should take some food in my pocket, the bigger torch...maybe I should take my rucksack with me — better not, I have to go back anyway, back to the laptop so I can write the whole thing down. I should not forget to make sure that the door stays open, though; I should always put a book or something in the doorway, just in case.

The fire is burning now and I have already had breakfast. I am going to write about yesterday's trecking, wait until the fire extinguishes itself, and then I will go back in — the faster we get to the bottom of this thing, the better.

A gust of warm air came out from the weird room. The room was not a dark hall any more; quite the opposite, now it was a very bright room, so bright that I had to close my eyes for a few seconds. I walked in slowly, with my hand shielding my eyes trying to see what was in store for me this time.

The light came from above, as if the whole ceiling was on fire. The floor was irregular, with small stones and bumps all over; it looked more like the ground outside than an inside floor. However, we were not outside; I could sense the room was enclosed, although I could not see its walls.

My eyes gradually got accustomed to the light, and after some time I did not need to cover them with my hand any more. It was getting too hot and I took my jacket off. I went back to the hall, left my jacket on the floor, placed a chair so the door could not be shut, and then I went back in. The whole thing was a desert, a rock desert under a big marquee with lots of powerful spotlights from the ceiling.

I waited for a couple of minutes to see whether any animal would come to guide me. This time I was left on my own. I walked a bit more and I waited a few more minutes; nothing happened. I was getting increasingly warm, and the light from above was annoying me, but by then I realised that I had to find whatever I was supposed to find by myself, so I decided to walk in a straight line.

I kept walking and walking but the only thing I could see was the open door getting smaller and smaller behind me. I did not want to walk so far that I could not see the door, so I decided to leave some sort of mark so I could come back to the spot where I could still see the door. I gathered some stones and I made a small pyramid with them; it was not very big, but I could see it from quite a distance.

When I almost couldn't see the small pyramid I made another one, and I repeated the process again and again. I could not find anything or anybody except for ground and stones. I had already taken my jumper off and I was regretting wearing that thermal long sleeved shirt — although I do not know why I kept it on.

I was doing something wrong, that was obvious, and the best thing I could do was to stop and think. Normally, I just go in and things happen by themselves. There is always an animal that either does something, or guides me to do something; but this time nobody was doing anything; there were no animals at all. A desert, no animals...then I realised.

I should have guessed that at one point I would be asked about extinction. I, like anyone else, share the responsibility for the species that have been made extinct, and especially the ones that will be extinct because of our direct or indirect actions.

I could not remember ever seeing any individual of a species that later in my life had become extinct, but the closest case was the two golden eagles in Cumbria.

I was on one of my hitch hiking trips to the North when I went to volunteer for a few weeks in a Lake District natural reserve. It belonged to a charity and the most important aspect of the work was to look after the last two golden eagles in England. We had to take turns to spend two–day shifts in a cabin about two miles from the eagles' nesting site. It was a beautiful place; a huge lake nearby, mountains in all directions, amazingly green valleys, wildlife everywhere, etc. We had to be sure nobody got close to the nest — by accident, or professional egg thieves — and if there were any visitors coming to see the eagles, we would show the eagles to them through powerful telescopes — ensuring this was as close as visitors would get to them.

Unless you knew a little bit about the area it was not easy to find the eagles from that distance. Visitors had the advantage of having us; they only had to wait for us to locate the eagles and tell them where to look. The daily routine was as follows: waking up with the sunrise, having some breakfast, using the telescopes to locate the eagles, radioing to the base to tell them that there was nothing to report, finding with the telescope where the eagles go, showing visitors their location, and going to bed (with the proper meals when required, of course). It may not seem much to you, but it was quite exciting because some days no eagles could be found; it was quite a challenge to spot them and to track them all day. That happened 24 hours a day, for the rest of the eagles' lives, and for the wardens'.

I remember when I first saw one of the eagles because it was my thirtieth birthday—at 12:55, to be precise. I spotted a dark figure on top of a rock in the middle of the eagles' valley—this is what we called it. It was difficult to see at first —it could have been just a tree stump—but it turned out to be the male—according to the more experienced warden that was with me at the time. I was so excited that I even drew the whole scene in my notebook, together with a diagram of the cabin, and a map of the site. It took me a few more days to spot the female, but at the end of my stay I was already quite good at it.

The experts said that those two eagles were going to be the last in England, because all the offspring they ever had flew north to Scotland, where the population of golden eagles is quite healthy. In fact, the Isle of Skye is one of the areas in Europe with the most wild golden eagles—I spotted one the other day, remember? That year the couple only had one egg—which failed—and the year before they only had two unfertilised eggs—the eagles were getting old. After a record of 200 golden eagles in Cumbria in 1969, these two were the last pair left, and nowhere else in the rest of England was there the 50 square kilometres of complete wildness that would be required to find another one.

The telescopes by the cabin were as close as I ever got two those two eagles—which, by the way, nobody had taken the time to name, or tell me about it. Most of the time, though, volunteers worked in other places in the reserve. I used my expertise to write an inventory of bees and wasps in the area, and I also did some translocation work of a wasp nest that was conflicting with the human population.

I do not know whether those two eagles are still there—I suppose they are, otherwise they would have appeared in the weird room with the others. The point is, why precisely those two? Why can people get close (even if they should not) to any of the Scottish eagles, but not the English ones? Do those two eagles know that this is why they are watched every day through the telescope? Do those two eagles know they are English? Are they?

Maybe golden eagles are going to be with us for some time, but maybe I have encountered other animals whose species will be extinct before I die. How do I know? How do I know that the tigers I have seen in zoos and their wild counterparts are not going to die before I do? Then, although I would have known a species that will become extinct, what relevance has my own death to the extinction of a tiger? If they get extinct after I die, I would have witnessed individuals of a doomed species anyway. For that matter, how likely is it that any of the species I have seen will not become extinct at one point in the future? Not very likely, is it?

Therefore, if most animals we know will be extinct in the future, is it really worth preventing the extinction of a particular species, the species we most like? Would it not be selfish to favour a particular species helping to delay their extinction if we have chosen the species because we like them, rather than because they deserve to exist? Is there any species that does not deserve to exist? What moral basis have we to protect one species from extinction more than another? Or, as in the case of the eagles, protect one population more than another? Is this a matter of national pride? Is this a matter of human pride?

Urgency is the factor we use to justify our species conservation tactics. If we are able to foresee that one species is more likely to be extinct sooner than another is, we help the first one. Following this, if during my life I have acted in such a way so as not to help the species that, with what I knew about it at the time, was going to become extinct first, I can then be blamed for its extinction, can't I?

I do not think so; delaying is not preventing. By helping the next species that is going to become extinct through delaying its extinction, what we are actually doing is to put the second species in the list as the next to get extinct. We are not preventing anything; but we are only delaying the process for some, and indirectly increasing the risk of others by not having used for them the resources we spent on the protection of the first one. We are playing with the species like somebody playing with a pack of cards; we are only shuffling them about, but the game goes on.

What if the way we assess urgency is not accurate, anyway? What if the way we label animals is not accurate either? In fact, species do not exist. They are just a way we classify living organisms. We call 'species' to groups of organisms we think are capable of breeding successfully among themselves, but we accept any exceptions if they are convenient to us, and we do not mind if they will never actually breed among themselves in real life. We make species extinct all the time by changing their names or by re–classifying them. We extinct and create species in the blink of an eye. The truth is, though, that it does not matter whether a species goes extinct or not, as long as all its individuals stay alive and well.

Credit should be given to the fact that the delusion of the concept of species, and the threat of their extinction, allows the introduction to people's minds of some ethical thought about what are we doing to our planet. This is true, but this cannot be the basis of a global conservation strategy. It is like trying to persuade a murderer to use a knife rather than a gun. I suppose the chances of the victim surviving increase, but this 'convincing' hardly qualifies you to become a police negotiator, does it? It is not enough, like sticking the label 'at risk' to a group of animals is not enough either.

The point of conservation should not be to preserve the Earth's species genes, but to preserve the Earth's species lives; to keep alive and well all the individuals, not to preserve their names or labels; not to preserve the ones at most risk, but all of them. When we start choosing, when we start selecting which pairs go into the Ark and which do not, then we start losing the point. It is not an Ark that we have to build; we have to stop the divine flood.

The weird room had no animals this time, but animals

were not the only thing missing; everything else was missing; it was a desert. It is not the lack of some species which matter about extinction, but the lack of life as a whole. In the end, the causes of extinction of various species are most of the time the same, and therefore the effect is more likely to be devastation rather than just extinction. The flooding water is the same for the panda as for the squirrel; the solution is not an Ark, but a dam.

I am not into saving 'the pure'; I am not a puritan. There are plenty of puritans these days; purity of genes, purity of body, purity of thought, purity of culture, purity of language... No, I am most definitely not pure. I have genes from all over the place (a bit of French, a bit of Iberian, a bit of North African, a bit of Roman...). My body has its history of excesses and 'bad' things have passed through it. Impure thoughts are not unfamiliar to my neurological pathways — is this jargon one of them? Culturally speaking, I am a British–Catalan hybrid, and my language, well, judge for yourself. No, I am not pure, I am a total hybrid, I belong to nowhere, I have no rights, I should not be preserved; I should be grateful for not having been put down — and for the miracle that a publisher has accepted my work as well!

Conservation should not be about saving pure breeds, saving pure species, or saving pure types. Conservation is about saving the whole thing, all the ecosystems, with all their species, with all their individuals, with all their needs. These include the French and the non–French, the pure and the hybrid, the common and the rare, the loved and the hated; these include you (all the 'yous' in the universe) and also me.

Where is this dam, then? What have I done to build this dam, eh? Did I climb any tree when a new motorway was going to destroy another forest? Did I refuse to use the genus <u>Polistes</u> to describe the wasps I was working with? Did I do anything to stop people breeding? How much time have I dedicated to finding alternatives to petrol? How much small print do I usually read in the supermarket? Have I ever thrown a soft drink can in the regular bin? How much paper have I used in my life? Did I do anything to find out how those two eagles are doing?

Guilt is not that heavy when everybody else carries the weight with you, but when the rest go on living, and you are left with the parcel alone, then it is another story, isn't it? I was the only one on that desert. That entire desert for me.

Chapter Fifteen
December 24th 2001

I almost did not make it yesterday, but I always do, don't I? Yes, it is still dark and yes, it is still windy, but now it is also snowing, just a little bit. Cold? I do not know, maybe a little colder—I do not check the thermometer any more, why bother?

During this entire ordeal I have often thought that I was dreaming—you probably thought it as well. It is not only the strange things that are happening to me, but also the way I react to them. If all this is real I should be terrified or I should have packed and run to the next village; instead, I accept any possible weirdness with an implausible openness, characteristic of the dream world. Yes, I suppose it is likely I am dreaming, but if this is the case you, the person who is reading this, should be part of the dream too, because these pages have been written in it. Hence, you must be as real—or unreal—as the rest of it.

Having considered this, I have tried to wake myself several times—if this is what you are thinking—but as you can see I have been unsuccessful—believe me, yesterday I tried as hard as I could. Because of this, the level of reality of the experiences I am living is totally irrelevant to me now. This is the world I have been pushed to live in, and I cannot run from it. I cannot honestly find any difference between the reality of my burnt rice, and the one of the hot desert; it is just another room, and even if every day gets a little wilder than the day before, I always manage to get out unharmed.

I opened the door slowly—I did not want to get startled again. Not much change in the temperature, no bright lights, no sudden surprises; just a horrible smell—I know what it was now, but I could not tell then. The room had returned to its original shape; the fireplace, the window, the old books...but there was no floor, nor anything that could work as a floor; instead, there was some liquid. It was as if the room had been converted into an indoor pool, but a sinister pool made of some foetid dark soup.

I stepped back, not because of the stench but because I realised that I was being asked to do something that I could not do. In the weird room there was nowhere to go other than in the soup itself; I was supposed to go in the soup!

I opened the porch door to pick up a lump of coal, and then I threw it into the pool; it sounded thick, it sounded heavy, it sounded deep, very deep. It was too deep, I could not do it, no way! I closed the door and I rushed back into the kitchen. I was petrified; the smell and the appearance did not bother me that much; the fact that it was a pool did.

I have always been terrified of deep water—no, I cannot swim, if I could the problem would be gone. I would not say that I was an aquaphobic (i.e. pathological fear of water) any more; the presence of water does not repel me, and if I am sure I cannot sink, I am happy to be on it—well, happy may be an overstatement here. The problem is the fear of drowning, and therefore the fear of putting my head into any liquid that could do the job. That horrible liquid could, most definitely could.

I sat by the fire trying to find an alternative. I could not be asked to do this; that was suicidal, that was psychological suicide. I had the sudden urge to pray, to pray for a change, for a modification, for a variation in the trial scenario; but to pray to whom? No, I was not thinking of God, I was thinking of the judge, whoever the judge was. Was it me? Was I the judge? Was I the persecutor, advocate and judge? Could I change the scenario? Maybe if I could think what the topic of the session was I would not need to go into the pool. This is how it normally worked, wasn't it? The room shows me a scene, I figure out the charges, and things flow from there.

What was the dark liquid about? And the smell, could I recognise it? I had smelled it before, but I could not remember where. Was it connected with my fear of water? Did my fear affect others? I could not think of anyone; I never found myself in a situation when any animal of any sort needed me to go into water to save it. No, I never faced a drowning animal, not that I could remember anyway —and I would if that had been the case —this was one of the rules of this purple world, I was sure of it.

The answer had to be in the smell. Maybe if I opened the door again I could smell it, and then try to remember. I went back to the hall and sniffed the door edges, but I could not detect anything. Keeping as far off the doorknob as I could, I slowly turned it.

Suddenly, the door opened itself completely, and, in a flash, a cascade of the liquid rushed out filling the entire hall. I was immediately thrown about, and the wave totally swallowed me. I was drowning; I was drowning in the thick fluid; I was drinking it and I was breathing it. I did not know where I was, I was pushed in all directions and I did not know what was up and what was down; I was dying.

When I thought I was going to pass out I was violently spat out onto the floor and the cascade of liquid came after me splashing everywhere. Struggling to survive, a jet of liquid came out of my lungs, and once empty I took a huge inhalation that echoed all over. I could breathe; I could finally breathe!

I was lying on the floor when the commotion stopped. The liquid was scattered all over and I could see it clearly now; it was red, dark red. I went on my knees and, still panting, I looked around. I was somewhere else, in a kind of circular pit, with concrete structures built all around it, enclosing it. I was in an arena, in a circular arena.

When I realised what this was about, what I was being accused of, I uttered a loud and broken howl that resonated throughout the whole place. That was not fair, that was not fair at all!

Since as long ago as I can remember I was totally opposed to it. Not that bullfighting had anything to do with the Catalan culture. In fact, it was very much a symbol of Spain—the National Fiesta, as they call it. When I became old enough to understand the political fabric of the world I was living in, my reactive anti–Spanish feelings were, I believe now quite excessively, extended to all aspects of Spanish culture, including flamenco and, of course, bullfighting.

Once democracy came to Spain, and Catalonia was granted its autonomy, laws were passed that made the use of animals in popular fiestas in Catalan territory illegal; nevertheless, some bullfighting rings were allowed to continue their activities—many Spaniards had immigrated to Barcelona, which happened to be the most prosperous city on the Iberian peninsula—as long as they were exclusively for the people who paid to attend. After all, many tourists coming to Barcelona looking for the Spanish stereotypes would pay good money to see everything they could not see at home, and Catalonians are known for their trading skills—if you get my euphemism.

I had a friend who liked bullfighting, though. We sometimes talked about it, and he used the typical arguments normally used to defend it; the bull prefers to die in the ring than in a slaughter house; it is one of the most ancient rituals known to humankind; matadors sometimes die in the ring also—and therefore it is a fair fight; it is an art full of aesthetic scenes, beautiful choreography; it is a popular cultural tradition among many good people; the bull is treated with respect all along; the bull that goes to the ring will live longer than a bull that does not; etc. I used to argue with my friend until one day he pointed out that I did not know what I was talking about because I had never been to any *corrida*. My friend was right; saying that I had never seen bullfighting in real life easily dismissed many arguments I was putting forward. I agreed, then, to go with him to a bullfight to witness it all with an open mind.

There was much more in the whole ritual than I had previously imagined by just watching it on TV, but I never had any doubt that the bull was suffering. First, he is confused with many people around waving capes; then lances are thrust into his flesh in order to make him bleed; then barbed sticks are stabbed into his shoulders to weaken his muscles and lower his back for the eventual kill; the matador manages to tire and confuse the bull by making him move continuously; when the bull is so exhausted that he cannot charge anymore the matador plunges the sword between the bull's withers; more often than not, it does not die with that, so to finish him off a dagger has to be inserted in the back of his neck.

I could not see art, I could not see respect, I could not see fairness, and I could not see acceptance on the part of the bull; I could not see anything that made that ritual legitimate in a society that would not accept throwing people to the lions anymore. I could only see humans cheering at the vision — and the smell — of fresh blood, after God had blessed them all in the mass hours earlier. That was the only time I went to a *corrida*, and I used what I learnt from it to reinforce my repulsion to it, and to the world around it.

I had always been, by all accounts, a strong critic of bullfighting, and of any blood sport for that matter. It was not fair; I had been thrashed about in a pool of blood for something I never did and never approved of. I did not encourage it, I was not responsible for it, and I always spoke against it. Just because I was born in Iberia does not mean I am a matador.

I stood up and looked for the door. I had figured out the puzzle and I had proven my innocence; I should be allowed to return. I walked around the amphitheatrical arena but the door could not be found. Was this a fair trial? Was this really a trial? If I could only walk away from a session when I had been proven guilty of a charge, what sort of trial was that?

Was that it? Should I carry guilt for the Spaniards and their bullfighting? I guess I should also carry guilt for the 'grey people' and their dull coloured uniforms. What about the Romans? I must have Roman blood in my veins too; should I carry guilt for their Games, for their Gladiators, for their beast baiting and for their crucifixions? Perhaps it is not only a matter of my blood, but also my new culture; should I carry guilt for fox hunting as well? After all, it is still legal over here, is it not?

Maybe I am indeed a matador, despite what I think. Perhaps I am a renegade matador who escaped the sword; or perhaps I am the bull who escaped it; a cowardly bull who escaped the fight. Maybe inside me animals and humans conference, as I know two cultures do, two different ways of looking at life. Maybe in my head no one holds the sword, both bull and matador face each other, talk to each other, and ask each other what are they doing. Maybe my sin is to ignore them, to run away from what they are saying.

What makes blood lose its redness, what makes death lose its transcendence, what makes compassion lose its 'defaultness'? People who went to see gladiators in Rome, executions in Kabul, bullfighting in Madrid, bearbaiting in London, cockfighting in Bangkok, freak shows in New York, or guillotines in Paris, they all enjoyed the experience in the same way, and for the same reason. They enjoyed the catharsis of extreme violence, humiliation and punishment and at the same time they felt the relief of knowing they were only spectators, not victims or attackers. These people still exist today, not just visiting the same events that sadly are still performed in our world, but also softer versions of them (sports, zoos, circuses, etc). They are not abnormally voyeuristic and morbid people; they are just regular people, with the same needs and feelings as the rest of us. They are, simply, us.

The truth is that it is easy to be entertained by torture; the only thing you have to do is to forget suffering, and we humans have a long history of this. Mass conformity and its reassuring effects easily override human empathy. Losing one's identity in a crowd also frees you from any residual guilt that may still be installed in your brain. It is much easier to enjoy the sight of suffering in a stadium, than to do it at home watching TV on your own. When popular mass torture becomes ritualised, there is not a drop of empathy left in our minds.

The explanation—but by no means justification—relies on the concept of 'survival'; people's anxiety at having been abandoned in a dangerous world, and the security regained when they safely watch the danger move away under the protection of their tribal crowd. It is a child's story, an Aliens' film, a summer's roller coaster, or a Circus's act.

I knew all that, and yet, rather than fight the crowd, rather than feed the sympathy, rather than stop the sword, I ran away to a land where the screams sound fainter and the blood smells sweeter. I looked away from the bull's eyes, and I ignored the fox that was staring at me from the other side.

The door opened. I left the ring with my head down leaving a trace of blood behind me.

Chapter Sixteen
December 25th 2001

Happy Christmas to you—oh well, you may be reading this at another time, I suppose. Christmas Day, such a nice day, when everybody is friendly, presents everywhere, good food, nice drinks, a warm fire, all the family together and, if you are lucky, you can even go out and play in the snow, can't you?

Well, good for you! I can also go out and play in the snow if I want to, you know? There is plenty of it; there is enough for all of us, for all the bloody people on the planet, in fact. Shame that it is still completely dark, the food is rubbish, I have no bathroom, and I am in the middle of a supernatural trial; but I still have a bottle of wine.

Don't worry, I can take anything; there's no limit. Everybody knows that I am guilty; it would be an extreme injustice if the verdict said otherwise. I only have a week to go.

I deserve it all, all of it; no, seriously, I do.

I went straight into the room and I did not even look at it; I just went in. Do you know what was in it? Furniture, books, a carpet...there was a room in the room! The same old weird room with all its bits in it. Nothing floating around, no creatures of any kind, no surprises; just the weird room as I saw it the first time.

Well, then, how is it possible that there is a full chapter written about it? Something had to have happened—otherwise this would have been the end of today's writing, wouldn't it? Yes, something did indeed happen. The door, the door behind me, shut itself closed and I could not open it afterwards. No, I could not open the door that leads to the toilet either. I was, literally, locked inside.

I thought about whether there was something I could conclude so far, but it seemed premature. The logical step would be to sit on the orange armchair, so I did; but nothing happened either. Maybe I should do the same thing I did the first day; turn the lights off, come back to the chair, and then turn the lights on again. I could try.

When I went to stand up I realised I couldn't. I tried to move my legs but I could not, as if I were paraplegic. I tried to touch my legs to see whether I could feel anything, but then I realised that I could not move my arms either—quadriplegic, then. I could move my head, but just from side to side—I could not move it up or down. I tried to move my fingers, but I could not either; I felt them, though; my sense of touch was still working.

It was time to think. A total paralysis, what can this mean? Was this connected to Chico, the paralytic monkey? I did not think so. Maybe it was more symbolic, as the lack of movement, the lack of freedom...

Suddenly, the orange chair moved, as if it had been pulled from behind, and it began tilting until it was completely horizontal. I could only see the featureless wooden ceiling and the lonely bulb — I felt uncomfortable in that position. My brain was thinking fast; I wanted to end it as quickly as possible; bulb...bed...death...

The nature of the ceiling changed, as if it were becoming transparent. I could see objects moving behind it, but I could not tell what they were. The chair, which was totally horizontal by then, moved upwards and began levitating towards the ceiling, as if it had been transformed into some sort of floating bed. When I got to the ceiling I went through it like a ghost, and I could see what was behind it. Metal objects going in all directions; flat long plates, curved tubes, rings...I could see their form, but I could not tell their function.

I was feeling really uncomfortable by then; I wanted to lift my head, but I could not; I found it difficult to breathe, and I was getting dizzy with all those objects moving around. There was a sound now, a continuous high–pitched sound, like the sound of squeaking wheels...light, metal plates, wheels, bed...a hospital, as if I were in a hospital being taken to surgery...hospital, surgery...

I went to Paris for a trip to celebrate the end of my secondary education. That was my first proper trip abroad, so apart from being very exciting and all, it had its own logistical problems; I did not use the toilet as much as I would have done if I had been at home. The result was that, back in Barcelona, in a few weeks' time I developed some pain in the abdominal area which, according the family doctor, was enough evidence to require urgent hospitalisation.

In the hospital I was asked to take my clothes off, a doctor examined me and took me to a room where I was given some sort of painkiller—all very quickly. After that, I remember being taken through several corridors in a half–conscious state; my appendicitis needed urgent surgery. I was not sure what was going on; I just remember the ceiling passing me by, and the sound of the wheels—yes, the same kind of experience that I was having in the weird room.

I woke up in the hospital room when somebody explained to me what had happened. The operation went well, and the doctors, who prevented a quite serious peritonitis in time, literally saved my live. I had to stay a few days on a drip and return for a while due to some mild post–surgical complications (an infected wound).

What relevance has this experience with my trial? Where are the animals? Where is the guilt?

The metal objects that had been frenziedly flying about suddenly stopped; they all froze in their spots, but the squeaking sound continued; it lost its repetitiveness, though, becoming a continuous high–pitched sound; less metallic, more organic.

I could see a reflection of the bed on some of the now motionless metallic objects. They resumed moving again, but this time very slowly, in a more ordered fashion, getting closer and closer to me. Some of the objects had obvious cutting edges and it looked as if they were going to be used on my body; I did not like what was going on, not at all. I was sweating, struggling to move, and trying to shout. Now, the high–pitched sound resembled more of a scream, a high–pitched scream. When some of the blades came closer to my face I could see my own reflection; it was the image of a restrained and muzzled rabbit.

How unimaginable the life of a vivisection animal is. It is not just the pain, the terror or the diseases. All these are part of natural life too; all animals have evolved with bodies designed to face and fight adversity, from the viral infection to the almighty predator. They have evolved to recognise it, to avoid it, to fight it and to survive it. All animals are descendants of a lineage of winners against all the forms of adversity Nature could present them.

No animal, though, evolved to face the life of a test rabbit, a lab rat, or a research guinea pig. When pain and disease become their main purpose in life, their main reason for having been born and being kept alive, Nature must have broken down and given up. Their brains, designed to make sense of a world where bad things can be avoided, must be unable to help them find any sort of peace; their tissues, designed to fight infection and expel toxins, must be unable to identify what is normal and what is alien; their bodies, designed to run, hide, fight or die when confronted with danger must be utterly confused when they are kept alive in pieces. These are the models we use for our research; these are the bodies we use to test Nature.

It is hard enough to accept this suffering as a price to attempt to cure our most dreadful diseases, but when it is used to produce a new shampoo, a new colour for a milkshake, or a new lipstick, it makes you wonder why the Universe has not already imploded into a world of chaos where logic is forbidden, and pain is not bad any more. To torture to save lives, to torture to save jobs, to torture to save time, and to torture to save cash.

All this happens behind closed doors, all this happens miles away from each of our everyday lives; we have no choice; all this is done before we know it, before we can ask, and before we can care; all this is done by professionals that know better; all this is done for us, for our health, for our pleasure; all this is done for a good cause.

I would be dead without those rabbits, lab rats and guinea pigs. This is the cruel reality; all of them were used to test and experiment most of the procedures and drugs that saved my life on the operation table that day. They had been used to learn about my anaesthetics, to test my antibiotics, to understand how my intestines work, and to learn about how to open up my body and keep it alive. They had been cut, injected, infected, sprayed, starved, dissected, mutilated, poisoned, gassed, drained, dismembered, and ultimately killed so I could be saved on that operation table, and in any other operations that life still may be keeping for me.

We could easily have learnt without them, but we did not. I could have survived without them, but I did not. They all died in pieces for me, and I never thanked them. I thanked the doctors, I thanked the nurses...I never thanked the rabbits. Nobody ever does.

Chapter Seventeen
December 26th 2001

I cannot go outside any more. The snow totally blocks all the doors and windows.

I passed by a mirror and I saw my face. I did not look good; I did not look good at all. I had sagging eyes, scruffy beard, dirty uncombed hair, and a very pale colour. I look old, dirty and ill. Where is this taking me? How deep do I need to sink?

I have lost all track of time. I do not know how many days have passed since I last wrote.

The room was empty; it had nothing in it; no furniture, no fireplace, no carpet, no pictures; completely empty. Everything was made of concrete, even the floor and the ceiling; a hollow concrete cube.

I knew immediately what it was going to be this time. I had been waiting for it, I knew that sooner or later it would come.

When I left the Sanctuary I was planning to become an

Animal Welfare and Conservation Consultant. I thought I had been to enough places and seen enough animals to begin living from the knowledge acquired with my experience, but before I had the opportunity to organise my self–employing plans I was offered a job by an international wildlife charity based in the southeast of England. Among other things, my post would include investigating places where wild animals were kept in captivity—mainly zoos.

This is how I became a Zoo Checker. I had been one for quite a long time because I had always 'checked' places with captive animals—in quite a methodical way, I should say—but I never thought that it would be a term used to describe such an activity; besides, I was now a 'professional', I was working full–time, and I was being paid for it.

The more zoological collections I checked, the more I realised that this was something that one could get better at with time. There are lots of techniques involved; how to film and photograph without drawing attention to yourself, how to get important information from a casual conversation, how to recognise the signs of poor animal welfare, how to find out what happens behind a closed door without having to do anything illegal, how to collect evidence that can be used in a legal way, how to write a report, how to process information objectively, how to develop a campaign from the results of your investigations, etc., etc.

My efficiency in zoo checking worked as a virtuous circle; the better results I had, the more zoological collections I wanted to investigate, and the more I investigated the better results I had. In the end, I have more than 200 collections under my belt, which range from traditional zoos to butterfly houses.

One of the things I learnt was the ability to 'switch off'. One of the methods I used to identify problems with captive wild animals was to empathise with them. Over the years I had developed a sensitive empathic skill that had its most spectacular expression in my work with wasps, and this skill was certainly useful to study captive animals. I could see that something was wrong by looking at the way they behaved and trying to tune myself into their perceptive and cognitive world. The problem was that, by doing so, I could be too directly affected by the ordeal the animal was going through, so to function properly and be useful I had to be able to switch on and off my empathic 'eye'.

It was through all these experiences with captive wild animals that I understood the true nature of zoos. In a zoo, if an animal is not neurotic it is frustrated, and if it is not frustrated it is exploited.

Zoos are monuments to human power over Nature; the human race is not only powerful because it can get under its control any animal from the sea, land and air—all of them—but also because it can treat its slaves with compassion, giving them the 'best possible' captive existence. Further more, it thinks it is able to recreate in just a moment any piece of land Nature took millions of years to evolve; and if the Earth is in trouble oppressed by the wicked and the ignorant, it will come and save it all.

We have chosen a society that aspires to give rights to individuals, to take animal welfare seriously, to stop the exploitation of the weak, and to acknowledge the importance of psychological wellbeing; a society with these values is a society against zoos.

The modern zoo's excuses and justifications do not work for me either. If a zoo today was only interested in making money by exhibiting its 'freaks', instead of working for conservation or education as many claim, what kind of things would it be doing? Would it deliberately display its animals in such a way that visitors could see they are suffering? Would it hide the fact that some of the species it keeps have turned out to be classified as endangered? Would it stop schools visiting just in case children learn something? What would it do—or not do—that would prevent it standing out from the crowd and being exposed by people that only dislike 'bad' zoos? It would change its image, it would cover up its intentions, and it would present itself as the saviour of the animal kingdom, rather than the exploiter. Just by looking at a zoo you would not know if its claims are genuine or are in fact totally false.

Is keeping, breeding and exhibiting wild animals away from their natural habitat really conservation? Wild animals are not pet toys, domestic products, laboratory subjects, circus props, or zoo exhibits. Their nature cannot be forced without loosing their wildness. It is not their genes, bodies or even their minds that we have to preserve; it is their wildness, their integration in Nature, their role in the ecosystem, and their chance to evolve naturally. None of these can be achieved in a zoo.

What about education? It would be very educational to organise school trips to hospitals to see people dying from cancer due to a bad diet, car accidents due to drunk driving, fatal injuries due to racial violence, or brain damage due to drug abuse. It could even be entertaining, with the patients explaining their stories, and their doctors performing interesting tests. Surely some Human (patient) Rights Groups would exert pressure against such institutions, but the hospitals would only need to put up signs saying 'Do not touch infectious patients', or 'Do not feed cardiovascular inmates', or simply 'Do not laugh when somebody dies'.

Being compassionate with baby animals is an instinct zoos do not need to teach—although they certainly use it; instead, zoos override this instinct by showing that it is OK to be compassionate with a baby and at the same time jailing it for life. Zoos do teach; they teach how to justify captivity.

Zoo animals are modern politically correct slaves. They are slaves of the education, entertainment and conservation industries. As with the human African slaves, they were first brought from 'the wild', then bred locally, and then kept by saying that we cannot live without them any more. Not much has changed from the building of the Egyptian pyramids to today. Now, we do pay the slaves who can complain—if they do so—and we keep the rest as pets, entertainers or trophies; but we still use them all, we still exploit them for our benefit, we still own them, and we still fight those who want to free them.

I have seen madness in zoos; I have seen it, heard it and felt it. I have seen hundreds of animals showing abnormal behaviour, such as pacing or rocking (also known as stereotypic behaviour) but I do not remember any that I managed to connect with, to empathise with deeply enough to imagine what it was like. I guess this is because there is no longer anybody there; the soul has already left the hopeless body; they are not people any more, as they were before when they were born or when they were wild. They lost their minds, they lost their lives and they lost themselves.

I wish I could have met the people that inhabited the bodies I saw. That chipmunk that was trapped in a never-ending loop — probably acquired in a wheel, but now performed without it indefinitely — being totally unable to perceive what was up and what was down; that llama whose neck twisted so many times that its muscles could probably fool any anatomist; that emu whose chest feathers had long since disappeared having rubbed its chest on a fence during its never-ending pacing; that squirrel monkey that was loosing all its food because it could not stop pacing even when eating; that elephant who attacked her keeper after a whole life of swaying in a concrete cell. Some of these animals had signs in their enclosures with their names on them, but the person behind the name had long gone somewhere else. Their world had failed them so much that they had to abandon it.

Some people may make you believe that if a red liquid pours from an animal's nose this is not bleeding but a natural way to excrete excess protein. The same people may make you believe that if an animal paces up and down in a cage all its life it is not behaving abnormally, but it is the natural way animals react to cages. Some people will try to convince you that rocking animals are in fact happily dancing; others, aware of the absurdity of the suggestion, will say to you that they are probably not dancing, although they might be. The wisest of all will stay away from you before you ask why that animal is eating its own tail.

If you loose a limb the pain will be enormous but it will be localised in time, space and causality. If you lose your mind the pain may be infinite. How can anyone dare say that there is nothing wrong with an animal lost for its entire life in a vicious circle of useless repetitive movements?

Yes, I did know a lot about zoos and captivity, so when I saw the hollow concrete cube I knew straight away that it represented a zoo enclosure. For an animal that has evolved in the effervescent tropical jungle, the mysterious deep ocean, the grandiose mountain range, or the never–ending arctic ice, the few plants, pools and rocks of its brand new enclosure will still feel like a hollow concrete cube — maybe bigger than before, but just that. No matter how big your enclosure is, you will always be by the fence that stops you getting away.

In my cube, in the weird room, the door had not appeared yet. The trial had to continue. I sat on the floor and I felt reluctant to think. I did not want to go out; I did not want to figure out my fault. I accepted my guilt, and I wanted to be left there. I had already seen all that I had done to animals in my life; I deserved the cube, I deserved the cell, I deserved the emptiness. I just did not want to think any more, I wanted to crouch on the floor and cry my soul out. I deserved all of it; I deserved it for life.

The room began shrinking, and a very low–pitched sound, almost beyond the human acoustic threshold, accompanied the whole process. I stopped crying for a second, but I still refused to think. Because the walls got closer and closer I crawled to one corner and I crouched even tighter. I was not going to think; if that was my nemesis, so be it. When all sides of the cube were touching my body I shouted as loud as I could. I was prepared to have it, to finish the whole thing right there.

It did not finish; the walls began crushing me, and the pain was unbearable. I wanted to die right there, but I was not going to be so lucky. The cube kept crushing me further and further, and my screams ran out of air; yet, neither my life nor my consciousness left me.

I could not take it any more, my whole being was soaked in pain, each and every fibre of my existence was being squeezed further and further but never got any closer to the end; there was no end, that pain was for eternity.

That punishment was too much, I did not deserve that much, I did not deserve it...they did not deserve it.

The walls stopped.

How could I be suffering in my hollow concrete cube if I deserved it? How could the pain be incapable of worsening if I deserved the punishment? It would be much worse if I were innocent; all my pain was no comparison with theirs. They did not deserve it, and therefore they suffered much more than my eternal crushing.

It is not the enclosure, the time, the visitors, the

diseases, the laughing, the shouting, the loneliness, the freedom, the boredom, the pacing, the concrete...it is not that; it is their existence. They are wild animals; wild, this is what they are, and this is what they are forced not to be. They are not ours, not now, not ever. They never struck a deal with us, as others did; they never joined us, as others did; they never approached us, as others did. They are the others, the other people who lived and fought their own battles without us; who felt created by their own gods that had nothing to do with ours; who were here before a speck of our identity was even pre– conceived. They do not deserve to be who they are not; not them, they are wild, they should live wild, and they should die wild.

I switched them off, that is what I did. Their pain was so intense that I switched them off. I said I did it to be able to work, to be able to zoo check efficiently, but I did not. I did it to avoid the pain. I am no better than the people that catch them and forget who they are, or the people that keep them and do not want to know who they are, or the people that watch them and do not want to see who they are. I switched them off in fear that their pain would be too much for me, but I will never be able to feel it as they do. No matter how profound that pain can be, it is going to be their personal intimate Hell.

The door opened.

Chapter Eighteen
December 27th 2001

I do not want to write any more.
I did not go into the room yesterday—I do not even know what was yesterday or what is today, anyway. The room did not seem to want me either —there were no nasty surprises luring me in.

I am deep down a hole of snow. I cannot even hear the wind now, or the house creaking. At some point the air will run out, I guess. Maybe not, I do not know.

There is no water; everything is frozen up; the light comes and goes. I cannot use the fire—the chimney is blocked. It's freezing.

I do not want to eat; I do not want to do anything.

* * *

December 28th 2001

There is nothing else in here other than the laptop and me. Everything else is gone. There is no kitchen, there is no weird room, there is no snow and there is no cottage;

there is nothing else; only me and the laptop.

I must have slept wherever I was—in the kitchen I suppose—and I woke up a few minutes ago in here. There is not even a table or a floor. The laptop and I are floating in the middle of nothingness.

I cannot hear any sound, not even the laptop fan. The light of the screen allows me to see myself; I am naked, I do not have any clothes, but I do not feel cold. I do not have my watch on me, or even my glasses; I can hardly see the keyboard.

Nothing is happening. I have shouted, but nobody replies—there is no echo, no indication whatsoever of where I am. I cannot move anywhere; there is nothing to hold on, nothing to propel myself with in any direction.

Maybe I am dead. Maybe it is the end of the whole thing. This must be the time of retribution. The jury must have been deliberating and this is why everything is quiet. I must be close to the time of the Truth.

* * *

Nothing is happening. Should I write something else? If the laptop is the only thing I have, it is the only thing I can use.

Hello.

Is there anybody in here?

Do I need to write anything?

Why am I here?

Am I dead?

Is this still the trial?

YOU HAVE BEEN ACCUSED OF ABANDONMENT, RUTHLESSNESS, VANITY, SELF–INDULGENCE,

COWARDICE, SLAVERY, CANNIBALISM, CARELESSNESS, INGRATITUDE AND APATHY TOWARDS MEMBERS OF THE ANIMAL KINGDOM.

(I have not written this, the laptop is doing it itself!)

YOU HAVE PLEADED GUILTY TO ALL THE CHARGES.

I see; this is the end; this is my end.

DO YOU HAVE ANYTHING TO SAY BEFORE SENTENCING?

Yes, I have. I have done things because I am a mammal, I am a primate, I am a human, I am male, I am adult, I am white, I am a westerner, I am Mediterranean, I am Catalan, I am a Scientist, I am a Zoologist, I am a Conservationist, I am an Animal lover and I am a person, but everything I have been accused of in this trial I have done it because I am guilty.

I have no excuses. I have treated animals as if they were objects, even worse, as if they did not exist, as if they were not there. Blinded by the delusion that I loved them, that I was helping them, I exploited them, I used them, I lured them into my perversions. I did not even realise how badly I was treating them. I cannot believe what I did! How could I...I treated them with disrespect, I played with their feelings, I tortured them, I murdered them, and I ate them! What kind of monster am I? How could I be so hypocritical? How could I...

I am guilty; I am guilty as hell of having abused them!

I am guilty...

I am guilty...

YOU WILL NOW BE SENTENCED;

THIS COURT, IN THE NAME OF ALL ANIMALS WHOSE LIVES HAVE BEEN AFFECTED BY YOUR EXISTENCE, SENTENCES YOU TO SPEND THE REST OF ETERNITY IN HELL.

APPEAL DENIED.

PART TWO

Chapter Nineteen
September 23rd 2001

I got the title while sitting in the third row of a small cinema in Penrith, at the heart of the Lake District. I could not say that it was a classic old cinema, but it did have something that made me wonder about reality, and the chances of being fooled by the lack of it. A mature woman was selling sweets with one of those trays you can hang from your neck; I have never seen one of those before, other than in films—that was probably a good sign.

Yes, I got the title there, but a few minutes before I got the main plot. No, it was not in the cinema but in the Italian restaurant. Sitting at the round table, in the middle of the room, I got the main plot when I was waiting for my *Spaghetti a la Carbonara*, my favourite. I had been carrying the idea for quite a long time, and I had been taking notes for over a year, but it was in the last months that had I decided I should transform it into a reality; I should write a book.

Recently, the writing became more and more present

in my daily thoughts, especially during travelling. My job made me travel quite often. No, I am not a sales man; I am a Zoo Checker. I check zoos; this is what I do. Well, zoos and any centre that could be defined as a zoo under British law (these are centres that keep wild animals and are open to the general public; a small aquarium, or even a butterfly house qualifies).

I visit them, and I check them. Am I an inspector? Well, not quite; I am an animal welfare campaigner, working for an international wildlife charity. I visit zoological collections, I film them, then we analyse the tapes and decide what to do. Sometimes we do nothing; sometimes we develop a specific campaign about that collection, and sometimes the information contributes to much broader research that will target general issues about captivity—and questions the need for keeping wild animals. In any case, we, and me in particular, end up visiting lots of collections, and travelling a lot.

It was last year when I thought I could write a book about my experiences with animals. In fact, it was then that I began writing some notes about them—mainly inspired sentences that occurred to me on a train or a coach. I do not know why, but motion always inspires me. I am the sort of person who paces all the time; I cannot help it—sometimes it worries me. It is as if I will fall into a coma if I stop. It is not just pacing up and down while I am thinking but it is the work as well. I cannot take breaks, let alone holidays. To me they do the exact opposite to what they are supposed to do to people; they stress me out—a typical sign of a classic case of workaholism.

It is precisely my lack of holidays that prompted the decision to write a book. Many work colleagues have been pressuring me to take some holidays. It is tempting to believe that they are worried about my health, but I have lived long enough to realise that it may be something else—nobody likes people that do not take holidays, because they make you question whether you really need breaks, or even if other people question whether you really need them. Anyway, I had been giving some thought about how to manage to keep working whilst giving the appearance that I am taking a break from work—so everybody is happy. The answer was to take a break in order to write the book. It seemed a good plan to me; the only question was to decide where and when.

As far as the 'when' is concerned, that was easy; Christmas time. Well, lets be frank about this. I know that it is politically incorrect—and generally very unpopular—but I hate Christmas. I do not think that this is the time to explain why, but I know that if I have to keep you interested in my story the least I can do is to be honest from page one. I am not a writer, nor any other sort of artist. I am a scientist with some stories to tell—if I do not hook you through honesty I do not think I have a chance.

Hence, it will be Christmas time, for a period of, let's say, one month—yes, I know that this is not much time to write a book but I cannot abandon my work for more than that; besides, I am a workaholic, remember? We can do wonders in a month.

I've got the 'when', but I do not have the 'where'. I have

some ideas but nothing concrete — as always, something will come up at the last minute. The important point is that I have made the decision to do it.

Getting a main plot as well as a title before knowing 'where' was quite a bonus, wasn't it? I thought that things had been set in motion, so I could not let the Universe down.

When the film finished I walked back to my B&B under the thin warm rain, and I found myself alone in the streets of Penrith at night. There was some magic in the air; it could have been the effect of the Sci–fi cocktail, or just the miraculous event of knowing exactly how to get back without getting lost — or having to check the map once. Whatever it was changed my mood, and when I got into the room I did something I never do; I did not turn the TV set on; instead, I turned the laptop on and I set myself the task to write the first page of the book — not too much, just a page.

Chapter Twenty
October 19th 2001

I just remembered it; I was at home warming up some fish fingers in the microwave when I remembered the dream I had when I knocked my head falling downstairs at work. When I was awoken by the people at the office and the paramedics I mentioned that I had been dreaming, but I did not remember what about. Well, I just did; it was about me writing a book.

I have had this idea of writing a book for quite a while, but I never found the time or the opportunity. I kept thinking of parts of it, what it would be about and all that, but they were all disconnected ideas that did not seem to combine together to form a proper book. A few weeks ago—after the head accident—when I was zoo checking up north, everything seemed to fit into place. I did manage to find a way to put the thoughts together, and I even wrote a little bit. Now it seems that the ideas I had come from that dream. I dreamt that I was in a cottage on the Isle of Skye, I found myself being put on trial by the ghosts of all the animals I have met, I was found guilty and then sent to Hell.

Immediately after the accident I remembered that I had believed the dream—which I could not remember then—was of great importance. That feeling made me write today—maybe it is some sort of premonition. Maybe I should go to the Isle of Skye to write the book. In fact I had already thought of some sort of animal trial, but definitely not about the 'Hell' thing.

It is funny, because although I already had the main plot of the book—the animals, the trial, etc—and I had already decided that I would write it this coming Christmas—we have an unusually long break this year—I had no idea where I could write the book. I only knew that it had to be a quiet place with nobody around, but with some character so I could get inspired. Now the dream has given me the perfect location; the Isle of Skye.

I am somehow reluctant to write more about it now—I do not feel very inspired anyway. I already wrote a page of the book a few weeks back, but I think that the best thing is not to write any more until I get to wherever I am going to write it; nevertheless, the fact that I remember that dream today justifies a bit of writing—who knows, maybe I am going to forget the dream tomorrow, and then I will lose the opportunity that fate just presented me. Do you think it might be any connection with the microwave?

I should make an effort to remember more about the place. Maybe I could try to find a site like the one in my dream. OK, I remember that there was a kitchen, the room was upstairs, and there was a fireplace in the kitchen—well, this is not much help, is it? There was also a strange room, but it was the bizarre part of the dream—I would rather not write about it now.

Maybe I should try to visualise the outdoor bits. There was a castle in ruins on the shore rocks, very close to the cottage; there were high mountains behind; there was a small forest on a hill just behind the cottage; the sea in front.... Ah, I remember the roof of the cottage as well; it was a corrugated–iron roof.

I cannot remember much more of it—it was quite a long time ago I had this dream. It was weird though; the end was more of a nightmare than a normal dream—maybe I am mixing several dreams here. How is it possible that I just remembered it today? I cannot find any particular reason.

Thinking about it this was not an ordinary dream, though. To start with, it happened while I was unconscious, not sleeping in bed; then, I remember it because it was a very long dream and I was out only for a couple of minutes; the memory of it is unlike ordinary dreams—I cannot explain why. Ah, and I remembered just now, after weeks of not remembering a thing. All this is enough exceptionality to take the dream seriously. Something interesting may come from this one.

Maybe what I should do is to get a map of the Isle of Skye and look for cottages that have a castle close by, a forest behind, and some high mountains around. I should follow my instinct, whatever it is trying to tell me.

Chapter Twenty–One

November 7th 2001

An amazing thing happened yesterday. I am still shaking about it; it is incredible.... I do not know how to put this—maybe somebody is making a fool of me.

I was working at home on one of the time sheets for one of my zoo visits when my laptop 'crashed' (i.e. everything stops working and the computer needs to be re–started). It is not an unusual phenomenon so I ran the diagnostic program that normally sorts out these things. It showed that the laptop had a computer virus in it—I have an anti–virus 'vaccine' program always in the laptop memory, and I always update it on–line with all the virus definitions, but this one somehow slipped through the net. My anti–virus software allows me to 'quarantine' infected files, so that they can be cleaned (i.e. delete the virus in them) and then restored, rather than delete the whole file from the start. Sometimes it does not work, but in this case it did.

The file recovered was a temporary file called

'~WRL3360.TMP', and it was dated 28/12/01. It was one of the *Word* (my word processing program) files that are created when you are writing a document, and they should be deleted once you have saved the final version and left the program. Sometimes, though, they are not deleted—mysteries of computing— and remain hidden on your hard disk (files starting with '~' are not normally displayed on the screen). The weird thing about this one is the date; we are in November; how can a file that is going to be saved in the laptop more than a month from now already be in it?

That is not all. I renamed the file in order to be able to read it with the word processor, and when I opened it I found something incredible. It was my book, the book I wanted to write—well, the book I had dreamt I was writing on the Isle of Skye when I was unconscious because of the head accident. How can this be possible? It is exactly how I dreamt it. How can it be somebody's joke if I have not told anybody about it? How can the book have been written if I do not remember doing it? How can the date of the file be a future date? What is going on here?

I have been thinking and there is one possible explanation; I wrote the book myself, and I have forgotten about it. I must have a serious problem in my head. I am the only person that could have written it. I spent all yesterday going through it and all the experiences described are totally personal, many never explained to anyone; and the ones I had explained were never explained in such detail. I was deeply moved by many of the chapters; they are very intimate views and events that touch parts of myself that nobody ever has reached. I am the only person that could have written it, and yet I have no memory of it whatsoever. As far as the date of the file is concerned, it must be a computer glitch, or perhaps one of the effects of the computer virus.

It must be me. There must be a problem with my memory; there must be something wrong with my memory. I have to go to the doctors soon. I will not tell anyone about this yet — first I have to go to the doctors and then see what he says. This may be serious, it may be a brain tumour or something.

What could have caused such extreme memory loss? Could it be the use of my mobile phone? I do not think so; I do not use it that much. Maybe it is the time I spend in front of a computer screen — no, there are no bases to conclude that either. It has to be stress, all that work and caffeine; or even better; trauma. It must be some connection with my head accident. Yes, there must be a neurological problem caused by the knock on my head. The fact that, after the accident, I had the dream about the same subject the forgotten book is about confirms the connection. Maybe it is not that serious after all; just a few neurones lost and some memories mixed up — that may be the end of the story, just a predictable side–effect. It feels bigger, though, it feels much bigger.

I had better keep a diary about everything related to this issue because my memory may get worse and then I may forget everything. It is important; I should be writing whatever happens to me. I should go to the doctor as soon as possible and then go back to the laptop and write.

Chapter Twenty–Two
November 12th 2001

My face looks symmetrical and my walk appears to take me where I want to go in a relatively straight line. I can pronounce everything with the same bad Iberian accent as ever, and with my glasses on I can focus on the world that is accessible to me. Yes, I have headaches, but I have always had them. Yes, I am quite useless with my left hand, but I always have been. No, all in all I do not think I can detect any neurological dysfunction that would support the hypothesis of a tumour; but then again I am not a doctor, so I decided to visit my GP.

I went yesterday—I had to register first because I have never needed a doctor since I moved to Brighton, and therefore I had not bothered to register before. I explained to the doctor about my memory problem but I did not tell him about the book; I just said that I forget many things, in particular work documents I am supposed to have written and that I do not remember.

He did not seem to take me very seriously. He was

looking at his computer screen asking me questions as if he was not listening to me. He seemed genuinely uninterested, I would say. Maybe he is like this with all patients, or it is me being paranoid?

In the middle of the session he moved some of the papers on his crowded desk and that movement slightly displaced several objects which eventually made a small pot fall from it, just in front of me. I quickly reacted and caught it before it touched the floor—I thought it was quite a fast reaction, wasp–like, I should say. I joked saying that at least it seemed that I had good reflexes, but he did not find that funny—I wondered whether it was done on purpose and it was some sort of experiment.

The doctor suggested I should take a blood test. I do not think that the test was to find out about my memory, but probably just to know about my general health—because I was a new patient and the computer showed no information about my medical history. I did not want to lose another day of work so I decided to go for the test the same day. Unfortunately, though, it was too late to be accepted in one of the two hospitals that do this sort of thing in Brighton, so I had to rush to the second one to see if I could get the test done there before they closed. I did arrive on time, but due to the fact that it was quite late and I had not eaten since the day before, I fainted when my blood was taken—no, I do not fear needles, it was just the lack of food.

I remember feeling quite bad when I woke up. It is funny, I have lost consciousness twice recently, and the experiences were quite the opposite. When I lost it with trauma and among pain, the lack of consciousness created a nice experience, whereas when I lost it in the comfort of a padded chair, the experience was bad.

Anyway, I have to wait for the results, and then go back to the doctor. I should pressure him to deal with my memory problem more directly. I should see a neurologist, I think.

I have been meticulously reading all the hidden files in my computer. Checking dates, looking for clues that can prove that I wrote things I have forgotten, etc. No luck; everything was accounted for, and all the dates were right.

I have read the book over and over again, and I am quite affected by the intensity of it. It does not show my style either all the time, as if half the book is written by me and the other half by someone else. It is quite disturbing; it is as though I had been in the Isle of Skye cottage rather than written the whole thing from imagination. When could I have written this book? It would have taken quite a long time and I could not have forgotten that much. All the events I remember fit perfectly well with the notes in my diary; there are no periods of amnesia there. I have no blank pages in my diary, and I remember doing everything that is in it.

The only way I could have written the book is if I did it at home in the evenings, but what kind of amnesia makes you forget only evenings? It does not make sense; it does not make sense at all. I should seriously consider the possibility that I did go to the Isle of Skye. Maybe what is wrong with my head is not the memory, but the logic; maybe I am mixing all these things up. Maybe I am thinking that we are in November, and in fact we are in January, and I am looking at the wrong pages of my diary. They are all blank after December 9th, as they would be if I had left the diary at Brighton to go to the Isle of Skye...but also as they would probably be if none of this craziness had ever happened. This is silly.

I am forgetting something important here; the dream. I had the dream in August and I dreamt about the Isle of Skye and the animals' trial. Then, in September, I had the idea of the book—I obviously remembered part of the dream without realising the connection between my inspiration and the dream. The next logical step would be to continue writing at home after I wrote the first page until I finished the whole book. Then something traumatic happened that made me forget the book and only the book—some sort of hysterical amnesia. Subsequently I remembered the dream—but by then I had forgotten I wrote the book—and finally I found the file in the laptop. The future date in the file is a computer glitch, and I am still under the effects of the hysterical amnesia.

With this theory in mind, I never have been to the Isle of Skye to write the book. Three questions arise, though; first, how can the book be so precise in the details of my travel and stay there? Second, what is the event that could have caused my hysterical amnesia? Third, since I only found a hidden file in the laptop, where is the actual book?

Regarding the first question, how do I know that the details are accurate? Maybe I have a better imagination than I thought. The only way to be sure is to go to the Isle of Skye and check the accuracy.

The amnesia does not seem to come from the book itself or the events in it. If I was mentally blocking out anything related to it I should have forgotten the book again after I found the file—I remember the book in the file now, so the book is not blocking anything. It is true that the book reveals to me many things I did to animals that I was not aware of, and this is in itself quite disturbing, but how can this guilt generate amnesia? If there is any amnesia at all it should be physical; it should have been something disconnected to the book—such as a knock on the head. If this were the case, though, I would have lost more memory than just the book, which did not happen—dead end there.

As far as the disappearing of the actual book is concerned, I could either have deleted it myself leaving the copy by accident—perhaps as a reaction to the event that traumatised me—or somebody else did it when I was under the influence of the trauma. I have no evidence whatsoever that anybody else is involved. The doctor does not even know me, people at work behave totally normally, and as far as I know there is nobody else around. It must have been me; but then again if I deliberately deleted it, it is because there was something in it that made me do it—I was denying the guilt that is expressed in it, for example— so we are back to the dead end.

Am I really guilty of all that the book says I am? Am I in denial of that guilt? Is this what all this is about? No, I am not. I accept what the book says; the descriptions of events are accurate, and the conclusions taken from them too. We have done, and are doing, terrible things to animals, and I am as guilty as anyone else is. I am not denying my responsibility; I am not denying my guilt. This cannot have been the cause of amnesia.

I do not seem to be able to make sense of all this. I only have one lead here; the Isle of Skye. I should buy a map and see whether the place described in the book really exists. I have no choice.

Chapter Twenty–Three
November 13th 2001

I have got the map. I bought two maps in fact, one covers the north of Skye and the other covers the south. They have the biggest scale (1:50000) I could find. It is going to take me ages to find possible sites.

I decided to look through the entire coast and see whether I could find any castles there. It seemed a much better method than to concentrate on the areas with trees, which, although most are marked on the map, it is possible that small areas are not. The castle option was the best, but the problem was, what did I mean in the book by 'castle'? There is not enough description to let me know whether we are talking about a proper castle or just a fortified settlement (what in Scotland is normally called a *dun*—I have looked it up in the dictionary).

There is also the issue of the island. In the book there is a description of a small island just behind the castle, and although there appear to be plenty of small islands all over that could reduce the possibilities, unfortunately, it turned out that it does not reduce them that much, since it seems that every time there is a dun, there are small islands around too. In the end, taking into account all the information I had, there were several candidates that would fit the description and could not be ruled out.

The question now is what to do next. On one hand pursuing the line of assumption that I did go to Skye and I did write the book is crazy since there is no time in my past when I could have done that — and I do not remember doing it either. On the other hand if I made the whole thing up — which would overestimate my imagination — I would still need to find the time to have done it, and it does not solve the issue of not remembering it either. Since the time travelling possibility is out of the question, the only handle I have here is the Isle of Skye.

What is all this? Why is this happening to me? Everything was going so well; this affair is totally inopportune. I had a very successful campaign on zoos, I was happy living in my little studio in Brighton, I was planning to write a book, and I had a very good idea of what was possible and what was not — more or less. I was content, I was happy with myself, and I felt proud of all my achievements. Why did everything have to be ruined with this 'paranormality'?

Maybe the answer is that I was too happy. The book is clear; it is clear about what I have done to animals even when I did not know what I was doing to them. The book is clear, and it has lots of reality in it. My life is totally exposed in there, and when I look inside I do not see fulfilment any more. If I wrote the book, if I was impelled to dissect myself and show to all what has been hidden, it is because my happy life was not real, it was a delusion. I had not been honest with myself and honesty pushed its way out.

Why did honesty have to kick me in the stomach, though? Why, rather than writing the book presenting the reality of my actions, and facing the responsibility they entailed by confessing them to the world, did honesty have to spit in my face with a mystery? Why now, after all these years, do I have to put myself on trial? Why do I now have to announce my guilt? Why, when I did it, did I forget about it? Why, when I have forgotten about it, do I remind myself again? Who is writing the script of my life?

Maybe I have been working too hard — people keep telling me. Maybe I should have taken weekends for what they are; weekends. Maybe I am getting old — what am I saying, I am only 37 — and I cannot cope with the rhythm of life as I used too. Maybe these things accumulate, and then your mind decides, without asking your permission, when it is time for you to take a holiday. Maybe I should take it easy, relax, and have a hobby — or something like that.

I should take a break and go to the Highlands to find the cottage. At the end of the day this is what I wanted to do originally in order to write a book — which I seem to have done already! Maybe I should go, and everything will be answered there. If there is something wrong with my brain the doctors will find it — it is obvious I cannot find it myself from inside it.

I should go; I should organise it and go.

Chapter Twenty–Four
December 29th 2001

The worse aspect about Hell is not that one suffers in it, but that nobody cares about that suffering. One's suffering is not exceptional, it is not particular, and it never ends or begins. In Hell, not even one's soul has identity. In Hell one is always anonymous, and cries do not have any meaning to anyone. In Hell one is totally lost, alone, and there is nobody else to share or blame.

Pain in Hell has no dimension, size or form; it is intrinsic; it is un–mutable; it is the effect of all causes. It is not like the fire that consumes through touch; it is not like the blade that divides the flesh; it is not like the rock that breaks the bone. Pain does not come from outside, nor does it come from inside. Pain in Hell is the fabric of one's existence; not a bit burns more than any other; not a bit can be crushed further than is already crushed. In Hell, one moves from pain, through pain, with pain, on pain to pain.

I, on the other hand, do not suffer. I do not feel the pain; I feel nothing; I am in Hell, in the heart of it, but I feel nothing.

There are many religions and gods, but just one Hell. They all think they know what Hell is; they all think they have the key to avoid falling in it, but they do not. No, the tortured souls that go to Hell do not end up in it because they have behaved badly; they go there for no reason at all. Such is the nature of true evil; everybody in Hell is innocent; nobody in it is punished; everybody in it suffers for no reason, for no reason at all.

I have always been here; I always will be; for all eternity, past and present. There is no escape, there is no outside, and there is no alternative for me. For a moment, I thought I could; for a moment, I thought I could escape, I could change, I could suffer my way out; but I was wrong.

I am not alone here. No, I am not, they are, but I am not. There are plenty like me in here. We all do the same and we always have done the same; we have particular styles, but we more or less do the same. This is who we are, we never question it, we never think that we could be anything else...and if we ever do, we will always be proven wrong.

I am a demon. I torture souls. I do lots of things to them. I cut them with knifes, I fill them with paste, I paint them with poison, I burn them with current, I hit them with canes, I stab them with lances, I strangle them with ropes...and if I feel like it, I play with them, I chase them around, I dress them up, I move them about, I put them in boxes...and then I boil them, fry them, steam them, burn them, smash them and then I start all over again. This is my job.

I do not really care about them, nobody in here does. They are nobody in here. When they come their souls are emptied, and from that point onwards they are just pain toys. We do not really know where one ends and the other begins. Our whole existence is based on torturing them. We are demons; this is what we do.

We demons do not go to Hell when we die because we already live here. We do not go anywhere; we are blessed and we have eternal souls so we do not die. We are the sons of the Boss and we are made in His image. We are allowed to do all this; we have to do this; from the beginning of time. We do not have free will, though. Mortals have, but this is not why they end up here; they end up here for no reason at all.

Something strange happened to me not long ago. I had a dream; I had a dream that I was not a demon anymore. I dreamt that I was one of them, one of the mortals. I dreamt that I could feel pain, that I had a choice, and that I had free will. I dreamt I could get out of Hell if I could show my guilt, but then it turned out that everything I had done was because I was a demon. It was just a dream; I cannot really feel what they feel. It was just a dream, a silly dream.

I have been thinking since that dream, though. I have been thinking about the inevitable order of things. We have a role in this cosmos. We are driven by evil, which is the main force behind us; the force that destroys; the force that separates. We have gone as far as we can go. We have freed ourselves from the causality of destruction. We do not divide to rebuild; we can now destroy for no purpose. We are aware of our power, and this awareness gives us the chance to stay away from fate, to avoid the extinction of the wicked, and to prevent becoming the tools of retribution. We know the ways of how to make our evil work unpredictable, our devastation undeserved, and our obliteration unstoppable. This is as far as we have gone.

I wonder where we are going from now? We have no choice other than to follow our destiny. We cannot change our evil nature; our will is not free. We shall continue with our destruction, and everything that had been together will rest apart. Total chaos is our destiny, and yet how can chaos be the end of a journey? How can chaos be predicted, confined, or aimed at? If evil drives us into chaos, should chaos detach itself from evil and prevent it achieving its goal? Otherwise there would be some order in that chaos.

If total chaos cannot be achieved, where is evil taking us? Can we go somewhere else? Can we change our destiny? Can we transcend into an evil–less creature? Can we choose?

No, we cannot. We can dream, we can think, and if our mind is tortured with doubt we can question, but we cannot escape our evil nature. We have to torture innocent souls. We have to break them apart until the only thing left is pure pain. We need to do it to exist. It is the most essential part of our being. We are demons and we live in Hell.

Chapter Twenty–Five
December 8th 2001

I have lost my scarf; the green one, the one that matches my gloves. It must have fallen out of my pocket. I keep saying to myself that the pocket is not the right place for a scarf; it is too small. I hate loosing things; this has never happened to me in the past.

Anyway, I went to a party yesterday; it was a Christmas party for everybody at work. I enjoyed it, it was very nice, everyone there together having a few drinks, talking about the past year and the plans for next one. Everybody knows that in few days' time I am leaving for my 'break'—they must be happy that I'm finally taking one. They all think that I am going to write the book. They do not know anything about the book that I have already written, and the mystery about it. Why should I tell them? What sort of explanation could I give?

Everybody was asking me what the book would be about. I only said that it is going to be about animal ethics—I did not want to give anyone too much information because I did not want anybody to suspect that something is going on. I wonder whether it has showed in my behaviour; it must have; how can I behave normally after having read a book that rips me apart showing how hypocritical I have been, and having been faced with a mystery that may be linked to having mental problems?

I do notice that I forget many things these days, you know? Minor stuff, but put into the context of the mystery, it may have some significance. For instance, I have never burnt more toast in my life than this year. I do not have a toaster at home, so I use the grill, but I then forget about it and I burn them all. Umbrellas, I lost one this year and one last year. I left a jumper in a coach too, which is something I never did in the past. I do not know, maybe all these cases are totally unrelated. The trouble is, how can one remember what one has forgotten if what has been forgotten cannot be remembered? I wonder how many other things I have lost which I do not even remember, or how many things I have done recently that I do not have any recollection of doing? Maybe the book issue is not an isolated case. Anyway, I hope that all these worries do not show up too much.

The important thing here is that I have found a cottage. It has all the elements; the castle, the woods, the island, and apparently, a corrugated iron roof. It was through a friend of the person that organised yesterday's party. I think this is the one, it has to be. The key element to finding it was the passage in the book about the mountains: "Trees at the back, sea at the front, hills on the left, and an abandoned castle on the right — with some impressive mountains behind it." I concluded that these mountains had to be the Cuillin hills, and since they are in the southern part of the island, the cottage had to be in the south–eastern quadrant of Skye (to have the sea in front and the mountains behind the castle, on the right).

Apparently, the cottage I found has not been used for quite some time. It seems ideal; I would have chosen it initially for my holiday if I had not been looking specifically for it. When I found it on the map I got a very strong feeling that I was on the right track. I am currently inclined to follow any hunch because my logic does not seem as infallible as it used to be.

Talking about brains, I had the blood results and they show I am high in cholesterol—what a surprise. As I suspected the test did not give any light into my memory problem, though. I had to remind the doctor about it again—he seemed to have forgotten—but eventually he did agree to arrange an appointment with the neurologist. Since mine does not seem to be an urgent problem—maybe he thought I would forget about it after a while—it will take quite some time before the appointment becomes a consultation. It is just as well, since I have already planned the whole Skye thing, and I would not like to cancel it because I have to go to the brain doctor—what would my colleagues think about that?

If the cottage is the right one it is obvious that we are dealing here with something other than memory problems. If it is the right cottage it means that when I had the knock on my head I dreamt about a real cottage. If I dreamt about a real cottage, I could have dreamt about a real experience too. In other words, I could have actually been there and have written the book. There is another possible explanation, one that I am reluctant to write about; my head accident could have temporally opened a window to the future—I know that this sounds crazy, I have been avoiding this kind of conclusion all along, but so far it is a plausible explanation, and I am not in a position to rule out anything without thinking. I did not forget anything; simply, it has not yet happened.

Let me elaborate on this possibility before I rule it out altogether. If the window to the future theory is correct, the problem is the laptop. I might have seen the future in my dream—some sort of premonition—but how had the file in my laptop jumped time? The date shows that it is a file saved at the end of December, but how did it end up in my laptop before? I do not know; this is silly. I cannot explain it; let's leave it like that for now.

There is something more that is preventing me sleeping properly at night; the trial itself. It is not the animal ghosts and the bizarre experiences—these probably are allegorical representations—but it is the stories about my past experiences with animals. Most of those events had been kept quite away from my everyday memory but reliving them through the book has made them surface too fast. It is like when you open a bottle of Cava and the sudden difference in pressure makes you lose half the liquid in an unstoppable jet of bubbles. A similar thing is happening with those memories; they all are coming out so fast that I cannot grab them, analyse them, and look at different angles or interpretations. They are all coming out and I am loosing them on the floor.

It is not that I do not accept the verdict; it is a fair one. I did treat many animals as objects, and I had the arrogance to go around waving the flag of animal lover and pretending to be fighting for their rights. All that I am accused of in the book are actions that were wrong and I am not proud at all about having done them — and having taken so long to face them. The problem is the sentence; it does not feel right. Not that I am trying to ask for 'clemency' here, or that I consider that what I did are minor offences and I should be allowed to be pardoned after having 'prayed' a few non–religious 'Hail Mary's'. It's not that; many things that were done cannot be pardoned by those who suffered them, and therefore anybody else's pardons are irrelevant. It is Hell itself; it does not feel right as a way of punishing my wrongdoing. It may seem strange but I believe the sentence is too lenient; going to Hell seems too easy.... I do not know exactly what I mean.

Anyway, tomorrow I am going to the Isle of Skye, a couple of days earlier than the day I, supposedly, went there as described in the book. I only need to follow the book and see whether everything fits into place.

Chapter Twenty–Six
December 30th 2001

I have been thinking a bit more about my dream. There was something that puzzled me. When I was dreaming I sometimes had the feeling of wanting to change something I had done in the past. Is this what they call remorse? We demons do not have that; every time we think of something we did in the past we do it exactly as we did before. Time for us is not linear. We do not die, we just carry on rethinking who we are; we keep repeating ourselves with no variation. When we think of the past, we go to the past, and when we think of what we did, we repeat what we did. We do not get older and we never were younger; we were created as we are now.

When I dreamt I had a past, I felt how being a mortal must be. Why do mortals have remorse? Why do mortals want to change the past that made them be who they are now? They are denying their own existence, renouncing their present. Why would you want to change something you did in the past, which undoubtedly allowed you to survive? Surely it is not the idea of Hell. Surely it is not

181

the actions you did that condemn you to Hell. As if Hell selected its inhabitants; as if Hell followed rules of justice and rightness; as if changing something you did in the past would prevent you going to Hell.

What is this thing about repentance? Why do some religions sell the concept that the verbalisation of remorse changes your soul? As if your nature could be changed by just remembering what you did. For us demons remembrance only makes us repeat what we have done. Our nature is unaltered by rethinking our existence. To mortals, on the other hand, remembrance is just a blurry vision of an unchangeable event that cannot be repeated, and therefore their nature remains the same no matter whether they think in the past or not. Mortals' thoughts are irrelevant. They have free will to choose any action they want, but they cannot change their past or their future. They cannot change their nature by choosing what to do, and it is their nature and not their actions that will lead them to their destiny.

Why bother with remorse? Why bother with repentance? I did not understand that in my dream. It is as if mortals are totally unaware of their nature and the order of things. I felt lost in my dream; I felt abandoned; I felt confused; I felt overwhelmed. I do not feel this when I am awake. We demons do not feel this.

What about responsibility? It is another of those things. How can an individual soul share responsibility with others? What is this concern for groups? We demons know that we are plural, that there are many like us, and each one has its own style and identity, but there is nothing we do that we do for another demon.

Our actions only affect the souls we torture, not other demons or their actions. We are individuals, and we live through our individuality. We torture souls on our own; maybe other demons torture the same soul, but we do not do it together, we do not help one another in our work; we just do it for our own sake, to fulfil our sense of purpose.

When I was dreaming I felt a sense of connection, a sense of plurality that went beyond quantity. I felt that mortals who had lived in the past affected my decisions, and I was affecting the future mortals with mine. I felt that remorse could occur when thinking of another mortal, not just thinking about yourself. I sensed that my destiny was decided by the group actions, not only my personal ones. How can this make sense? How can one be part of a collective and at the same time have free will only for oneself? How free is someone's will if it is limited by the uncontrollable actions of other members of the collective? How can mortals, believing that they live collectively, still think that they are in control of their destiny? Surely they can choose their actions but it will be the group that will choose their destiny? The group destiny will not be decided other than by the group nature, and this is beyond the individual mortal's control. How it is possible they do not see that?

Our existence is better. We do not fall into those stupid contradictions. We torture mortals for no reason. We always did it because it is the nature of our individual identity. Mortals are to be tortured and demons are to torture them. We cannot change the fabric of reality.

Good and Evil have to be in constant balance creating

and annihilating each other. They do depend on each other to allow reality to exist. Good joins and Evil separates. You cannot join something that is not separated, and you cannot separate something that is not joined together. Existence is the Good and Evil duality and reality is its struggle; gods, angels, demons and mortals are just the pieces of their game. We know how our pieces move; mortals do not.

Chapter Twenty–Seven
December 10th 2001

I am in the cottage, and this is the one; it is not only the place described in the book, but it is also the place I remembered in my dream. This is it; I knew that my intuition was onto something. Now things are quite different.

I arrived the day before I am supposed to have arrived in the book — I wanted to give to myself a little bit of time for acclimatisation. I do not know what I have to do. Would events happen to me exactly as they are described in the book? Should I write the book again? Should I write another book instead?

The overwhelming reality is that there is something paranormal in this. There is no memory problem that can explain the whole situation. I have been here before, I remember the place, and I know where things are. For example, I knew straight away that the main key to the water supply had no tap, so it only can be turned on by using a monkey wrench. I knew exactly where to find that monkey wrench — the owners of the cottage supplied none of this information to me, and the book only mentions the problem. Another example; I knew that to operate the gas I had to open the valves on both gas bottles, not just one despite the written instructions—that was not in the book either, but I remembered it.

I remember the silence, I remember the sunsets, I remember the cold, I remember the texture of the oak chair, I remember the smell of the corridor, I remember the feeling of the electric blanket switch, and I remember the colour of the trees. I have been here before; I have definitely been here before.

Hence, if that is the case, it is likely that I wrote the book when I was here. The big question is; did it happen in the past or in the future? I tried to remember whether I had broken anything or altered anything in such a way that I would be able to check it now, but I could not recall anything useful. I guess that the only thing I can do now is to wait for tomorrow and see if events unfold as described in the book.

Talking about the book, there are a few issues that have been playing in my head. What is the point in remembering something you did wrong in the past, and then accepting that you were wrong? What is the point of repentance? Does it make me a better person to recognise my mistakes? Many would think yes, but does it? In what way is the recognition of my mistakes going to prevent me making them again?

Today, for instance, I had a tuna sandwich. I opened the can—as I always do—I ignored the label—as I always do—I took its contents out without even noticing that it was fish flesh that I was spreading on my bread, and I ate it thinking of something else. I had already read the chapter about vegetarians and eating meat, I had already accepted that I was wrong, but what do I do? I ignore it completely and return happily to my normal routine. Is this learning from your mistakes? What had the repentance I had written (or read) in the book done for that tuna fish?

It is the Hell sentence, isn't it? How threatening could Hell be for an atheist? How much of a deterrent could spending eternity in Hell be for somebody who does not believe in an after life, as in the sense used in most religions? Not much, is it? Choosing a Catholic punishment was a very convenient decision on my part. What I have done with the book (or will be doing) is just a confession, a traditional Catholic confession, not to any priest in particular, but to all priests of the world, to all priests of all religions in the world; and what is the result of that confession? Is it reciting a few hundred Holy Fathers? Is it going somewhere on my knees for a year? Is it flagellating myself at night or wearing pebbles in my shoes? Oh no, all that would be too inconvenient for my busy life. The result is to pay later, in the afterlife; pay as much as I can, pay with an eternity of pain, but in the after life; not in this life, but after it. What am I, a philosophical con–man?

So, what is the guilt thing in the book then, just a way to get rid of it, to bury my responsibility in Hell so it does not bother me anymore? Is this why I have forgotten about the book, about having been here? Is it because I freed myself from the guilt, the mistakes, and even from the confession itself? Priests cannot tell anyone about what has been said to them in confession, can they? How practical! And I have done it up here, where there is nobody listening. Well, if this is my cunning plan to get away with it, it did not work. I am here, and I am going to get to the bottom of it, even if I have to go to Hell to do it.

Chapter Twenty–Eight
December 11th 2001

My laptop does not look as sparkling and futuristic as when I bought it. It seemed so slim, so cool; with the silver coating, the touch pad, the infrared port. Now it looks fat and slow, and the silver is falling off all over the place, as if it were cheap make–up—and I am still paying for it. You started the whole thing with that bloody file, didn't you? I know, it is not your fault, old chap. It is me, me and my funny head.

Today is the day. I have been in the cottage all morning—I do not want to leave it and miss something. The day is sunny, with not a single cloud in the sky, as in the book. I have been thinking about the actual time when I am supposed to arrive at the cottage today. It is not specified in the book, nor do I remember it myself from the dream, but it could not have been before midday if I had to buy all the food and stuff; so, I anticipate that in a few minutes I will enter into the book's time frame.

What should I do if things start being the same as they are written? There is something I have not been writing about that is making me nervous the more I think about it. Let's say that events start to happen as in the book. What about the trial? I may be here writing about the trial, or alternatively I may be here going through it, and writing about it afterwards. What if the bizarre and paranormal phenomena that happened to me in the book are going to happen to me again? What about the weird room? Yes, I have seen it, and I remember it as it is. Yes, it is weird, but just that. What if it turns out to be the paranormal portal that I describe in the book? Do I want to go through the whole thing again? Do I, ultimately, want to be tortured and sent to Hell? No, I definitely do not want that. If events from now on start to unroll as in the book, I have to see how I can alter them. If everything happens and cannot be changed, I am out of here.

If I am getting paranoid, if I am going mad, or if something is wrong with my brain, I should not be up here anyway. I need some answers, though; I cannot leave this mystery unsolved, otherwise I will definitely go mad. I will get some answers, and if a world of craziness opens up to me, I will go home and look for help. This is serious; this is serious stuff indeed.

**

It is mid–afternoon and the sun is beginning to set. Nothing special has happened. I am checking the book page by page and the book says that during sunset I sat in the armchair and had a cup of tea. Well, I am not doing it, am I? The silence does not feel so vivid—I arrived yesterday, anyway, so I have already been exposed to it—but it does feel weird. How can I feel normal? I am in the middle of an isolated cottage trying to figure out whether or not I jumped through time; and I should not feel weird about it?

It is much colder now—as in the book—but that is hardly surprising either. Should I light a fire? Why not, it is not through events that I have control over that I will find out whether I have already been in this time and place. I think I can light a fire without messing up with the experiment—I do not know what else to call it. The cottage does not seem warm enough, though; condensation can still occasionally be seen coming out of my mouth.

My stomach is not very well today—it may be that tuna sandwich I ate yesterday, plus the tension of the situation. Maybe it is my guilt that prevented me digesting that tuna properly. Maybe remorse does work after all, although in mysterious ways. If tomorrow I prove to myself that there is no paranormal phenomenon here—just a strange case of amnesia that is difficult to explain because I am the person suffering it—I should re–write the book. I should try to find a better sentence for my sins. Is that what they are, sins? Not mistakes, errors or bad judgements, but sins?

What is a sin, anyway? Let's check the Oxford Dictionary on my laptop: "sin, *noun*. (1) An immoral act considered to be a transgression against divine law: *a sin in the eyes of God* | [mass noun] *the human capacity for sin*. (2) An act regarded as a serious or regrettable fault, offence, or omission: *he committed the unforgivable sin of refusing to give interviews.*" It seems that a fault is a sin if it is regarded as serious by someone, including God. It will be a sin if it is seen as bad, not if it is intrinsically bad. If I had kept my experiences to myself, if I had not analysed and found faults of moral judgement in them, they would probably not be regarded as serious by anyone, either because they would not be known — is there anyone at work that knows I decapitated a live rat? — or because they would not be seen in my perspective — is there anything wrong with having a pet? I 'confessed' my faults and they became sins. The result, then, is major judgement; a sin cannot be forgotten, something has to be done about it.

Let's take the 'original sin' — Adam eating an apple — for example. It is not the fact that eating apples is intrinsically bad, but the fact that it was seen as bad, in this case by God. The result is that Adam and Eve are cast away from Eden and they become sinners from that day on — and so do all their descendants. How much of that punishment is the responsibility of Adam and Eve, and for that matter us, their descendants? Adam and Eve accepted the punishment, and so do we. Why did they, though? It was just an apple, after all. Why did they not argue with God showing that He created beings with a sense of justice? Is obedience more important than fairness?

The Adam and Eve story may have some parallels with the real beginning of human kind as it is now — which my book mentions in its initial chapters. Maybe humans, by going north from Africa, by leaving the real Garden of Eden of their own will, found themselves in such a different world that the pressure to exploit their environment — rather than to use it in a balanced way — increased. That made them start using and keeping animals in an exploitative way, as a method to survive in the new harsh world. That use of animals got out of hand, and mass agricultural practices began — perhaps it was not an apple, but a goat. The question is, can humans return to the Garden of Eden of their own free will? Can humans leave the original sin behind? Can humans abandon the outrages of overexploitation of Nature?

The issue of sins seems to me more linked to obedience than to ethics. When the Spanish Inquisition tortured alleged witches was it not confession — and repentance — that they were after? When the repentance was achieved, were the witches burnt or set free? I never got this one right. If the Church always forgives a repentant sinner they should not be burnt; if the way to prevent pain and death was confession — even of something not done — why not confess? If sins were about obedience, though, forgiving repented sinners would not help to achieve an obedient society, which was probably the real goal of the Inquisition. The order given has to be obeyed, and recognising that you have not done so it is not enough. Another example is executions in modern society. Has repentance anything to do with the fate of prisoners on death row? It does seem that despite having repentance as a way to achieve some sort of easiness in the after life, you will be asked to pay for your sins in this one.

In my book, though, I escape punishment. I do not pay for any of my sins in this world, but in the next one. I confess my wrongs — and I therefore make them sins — but I only allow my ghosts to judge me and to punish me in the supernatural world, not in this one. I do not accept a punishment in this world because the trial is kept secret until it finishes—and even then I still attempt to keep the secrecy...unless I am sent to Hell now, not when I die. Maybe this is the real punishment; Hell before death; Hell in this life. Is that what I sentence myself to? Is that what the world is sentencing me to? Maybe I am not trying to get away with it as I thought; maybe it is just the opposite. Maybe I am ensuring that I will not get away with it any longer. Maybe I have underestimated the power of my guilt.

Chapter Twenty–Nine
December 12th 2001

It is zero Celsius and the sun is up and shining. I cannot see any clouds. The kitchen smells of burnt wood. I am slightly tense and I have not slept well. I do not have much time to write now; I am going out to follow everything I did in the book.

**

I have been out for most of the day. It was an important day to clarify the situation.

I first went around the cottage, to the small wood behind it, to be precise. I was quite nervous because I was going to face the possibility of finding the red grouse and the hare I encounter in the book. I walked very slowly, looking everywhere. My heart was pumping faster than usual and I could feel the tension all over my body. Suddenly, just behind me, a loud flapping sound almost gave me a heart attack. I ran away as fast as I could without looking behind, I went straight back to the house, and I tried to calm myself down by drinking some water.

That could have been anything, it did not need to be a ghost; that could have been any animal—in fact, that could have been a couple of red grouse flying away from me. I looked at the time and it was 10:30. The chimney, I had to check whether the sun was touching the chimney! It was, but then again I could have deduced that by the geography of the area—I know I can make this sort of deductions.

After having relaxed myself I did walk to the village—yes, it did take me about an hour—and I did check the phone—no cash accepted, as in the book, but it could have been a permanent state rather than an event, so that was not conclusive enough. What was more difficult to explain was the old lady I passed by going to the village. That was too much of a coincidence. I said 'hello'—just to try to break the scene— and she just smiled at me and said nothing. At least, that was not identical.

The main proof should come from the sheepdog house. I was looking for a house with dogs all the way to the village, but I could not see any. I did not remember that scene at all from my dream, so I had to rely only on the book—which I had printed and taken with me. On the way back I couldn't see a dog either, and that definitely was against the book; instead, I saw another villager walking along the same route as me, a few hundred yards ahead. That was reassuring, things were looking different now; no dogs and a man walking.

I caught up with the man, and I said hello to him as well. He seemed nice, and his face was familiar to me—although I could not remember where I could have seen him. I thought that I might have met him when I came first time—now everything looked more as if I had come here in the past, rather than in the future/present—so I hesitated for a moment, wondering whether I should ask if he remembered me. I decided to talk to him, but in doing so I realised he did not speak English, but Gaelic—or this is what I thought it was—so we did not understand each other. I had heard that people up here in the Hebrides still speak Scottish Gaelic, but what I did not know is that some do not speak English. Maybe they do, but they do not want to speak it with strangers—fair enough, it is their land after all.

I went back to the cottage and I checked both time and temperature. It was 15:30 when the sun went behind the hill; so I went outside. Like yesterday it was already quite cold. A few hours before I recorded as much as 15°C, but now it was 4°C, as in the book. The sunset was beautiful, but it is always beautiful up here; no surprise there.

My conclusion so far is that the events of the book did not follow the events of the day. There were plenty of coincidences and similar things, but I suppose life does not change much up here. As far as the temperature and the light are concerned, I either came here in another winter, or I just made the necessary corrections and extrapolations.

I feel much better now. It is as if I had managed to take Hell off my shoulders—literally. Still there is the problem of not remembering when I came here to write the book, but this is a cake much easier to digest.

This basically means that the whole thing about being sent to Hell for real is not a concern anymore. The worry is now that I deleted—and then forget—the book after I sent myself to Hell in it, and although I vaguely remember writing it, I do not remember deleting it. What happens after having written the book remains a complete mystery. Maybe the solution depends on what Hell is for people like me.

If Hell is the representation of the worst that can happen to anyone, and one 'symbolically' sends oneself to it, there may be something very wrong in the way one judges 'good' and 'bad', or better and worse. Where is that survival instinct that has evolved with us since we were a lump of selfish molecules? If that instinct goes wrong, everything else does too. Do I have a defective survival instinct that made me write the book, or do I still have a functional one that made me forget it? Was writing the book a good thing to do? Was it right to put myself into a trial in which I represent both the accusation and the defence? How fair can a trial be if the judge is also the accused? Can humankind judge itself? Maybe this judicial incest does not lead to good. Maybe this is the beginning of the spiral that makes people lose their most essential control mechanisms. Maybe this spiral makes people lose themselves. Maybe this spiral makes people throw their lives away. Maybe this spiral does end in Hell.

Chapter Thirty
December 13th 2001

Things have changed radically, I did not expect this to happen, and I do not like it.

I was quite relaxed this morning so I decided to go and check the castle—I wanted to keep checking the book for coincidences and it seemed the right thing to do today. When I left the house I felt something at the back of my neck, as if somebody was watching me from the woods. I went there to have a look but I could not see anything. The feeling of being watched persisted, so I decided to go straight to the castle.

The ruins were very much as I remembered them from my dream—or as I was now convinced, my previous visit. No sheep this time, and that was good news. Indeed, the wooden bridge was missing, but you could still get into the castle if you walked on the narrow stone edge that once supported the bridge. I went in, and looked around, but when I was inside I felt watched again. I went to one of the sides of the castle to look around and then I saw a figure watching me from the distance. I took my binoculars out and I had a look; it was that man, the man I found when I was walking home from the village; he was there, looking at me with his binoculars.

I waved to him, but he did not wave back to me—I guess he did not recognise me. I left the castle and went along the shore rocks to the other side, where the island could be seen closer. I did remember the island with its seagulls and cormorants—no mergansers there, though. After a short while walking among the rocks I saw the man again, now sitting down on a rock looking at the scenery.

He looked at me and I said hello, but this time he did not answer me at all, not even in Gaelic. I thought he was a bit rude, frankly, so I went on my way and tried to ignore him.

He stood up and followed me, but then stopped, picked up his binoculars and pointed them somewhere behind me. I took mine and I looked in the same direction. My jaw dropped in disbelief. There they were, the two otters playing, as in the book. I could not believe it; in the same spot—but then again that may be their favourite spot.

I took the pages of the book referring to today and I read them again: "I followed it with the binoculars and eventually I saw the head of a common seal popping out; almost simultaneously the otters showed up again—I did not know who to look at, the seal or the otters. Beside them, in the sky, a golden eagle flew by. How much luckier can someone get!" With my heart pumping a bit faster I took the binoculars and I looked around for any sign of any seal. Nothing for some time, but then the seal appeared...and the otters...and the golden eagle.

I put my hands on my face in disbelief, and I waited to hear what I did not want to hear. A few seconds later the sound of two jets broke the silence. In panic, I ran away to the cottage, while I could hear the gulls calling in the background.

I am here now, in the cottage, and as you can see things are quite different. Today's events could not have been a coincidence. Yes, I have been here before, but not just in this place, but also in this time. What disconcerts me is that not all the events are the same. Yesterday's dogs, for example, today's sheep, that man...is this something to do with parallel universes?

Maybe some things are the same but others are not because I am not really in the same place, but in a very similar place. I could not have been in the same universe twice in the same time, it would have created a time paradox (all that thing about travelling back in time, seeing yourself, and killing yourself which makes it impossible for you to have travelled back). If any sort of time travel exists it cannot be in exactly the same line of time, but rather in a similar line. Everything has to do with quantum mechanics; the existence of multiple parallel universes can be deduced from the uncertainty of phenomena at the very fabric of our reality, where the laws of Nature are governed by probabilities rather than absolutes. At quantum level (which concerns the behaviour of the smallest particles this world is made of) all events are possible, so a world of multiverses seems more plausible than a single universe.

All very well, but the point of being parallel is that each universe does not touch (interact) with the other, so as far as any individual in each universe is concerned, they only live in a single universe with a single time line. Have I broken this time line? Have I jumped from my former universe to the next, where things are almost as my former one, but not quite? Have I, in doing so, landed in a slightly unsynchronised time? Was my knock on the head the event that made me jump?

Hold on, I heard a noise; I think it's outside.

* * *

The man, the man is here! I went outside with the torch to see if I could see anyone, and then I looked through the weird room window and the man I saw this morning was sat there, reading some books. He looked at the window, so I turned the torch off. I went inside, I took a piece of wood from the porch and I prepared myself to open the weird room door. When I did, there was nobody in there. I looked in the toilet, the rooms, everywhere; he was gone.

I have been around with my stick all over the cottage again and again, but there is no trace of him. He must have left through the rear door, for which I do not have a key—and it was locked when I checked! I bolted all the doors and I sat down to write this—What else could I do?

Why is that man everywhere I go? What does he want from me? Does he have anything to do with all this? Does he know anything about the book?

Wait a minute.... No, it can't be...the book...Oh, no, it cannot be!

Chapter Thirty-One
December 14th 2001

This is crazy; I have lived twice the time I am living now, and I am seeing myself doing it. What should I do, pack and run away? In a few hours some other version of myself is going to go to the weird room. What should I do, let him go in? What if the animals appear? Should I not care about it, and just run away as fast as I can from this madness? Who are the animals, anyway? It seems I was one of them — at least for him — so why not accept they can be somebody else?

This may be a real trial and some forces of Nature, which I am totally unaware of, are running it. The entire world I solidly constructed with all my years of asking and searching has now crumbled like a house of cards. I do not know what is real and what is not, what is fact or conjecture, or what is likely and what is possible. I can figure the whole thing out, though. If I think and analyse all I know I may be able to understand the new rules. After all, I lived all my life unaware of all these other aspects of reality. Surely I should be able to take better decisions now that I know about this.

It is still possible that no animal will appear in the weird room and that all that is part of the book my other self is going to write. Maybe these two parallel worlds are so close to each other that some entities in one 'resonate' in the other as different creatures. He sees me as a sheep and I see him as a different man—but with some familiarity in his face and manner. At other times, we do not see one another at all—maybe this is what ghosts are all about.

If I go now, I will never know if what he has written in the book is just fiction or some sort of reality. If it is some sort of reality, can it affect me or only him? If I am also involved, I might end up in the same Hell he is going to. If it is only his ordeal, should I let him fall into it? Is it not true that he is some part of myself, anyway? How does the survival instinct work in these cases? I think I should stay and see, at least to find out.

I have not seen him yet, he must be writing the book somewhere, in some other dimension or something. The cows are here, and so is the dead rabbit—no, I have nothing to do with it, and I do not want to know right now. Apart from that, everything looks quiet and I should try to relax as much as I can—and eat something if my stomach allows me.

What should I do in the evening? Should I go into the weird room and see whether he and the animals appear or should I watch through the window? If the animals appear I do not know if I could take it. I am going to look through the window. I am going to pack, just in case, and then I am going to look through the window.

I have been outside looking into the weird room for ages but I could not see anything —I am really cold now. I keep going in and out but nothing is happening. I left the light in the room on, but it was never turned off and on again, as far as I know. I do not dare to go in; I think I am going to bed in a short while—it is quite late already. If it is happening, it is not happening in this universe, and in this one I could catch pneumonia.

Just one last thought before I go. This man, my other self, is he me? Do his sins count as mine? Do mine count as his? I do not think so. We were both the same, but we departed from each other, and now we are on our own. We are not total strangers, though. We are closer than any two people can be. What happens to him is mainly because of who he is, and because of where he is. We are very similar, and we are both here, so it is extremely likely I will follow the same path he followed. We are bound to react to events in the same way, and whatever ghosts are in his mind, are also in mine.

If he has been put on trial for what he has done, I will be put on trial too for the same reasons, and if he has been found guilty, how can I not be found the same? I did what he describes in the book, and I would defend and accuse myself in the same way. If Hell is his destiny it is also mine, and I should try to escape this trial as much as I can.

If, on the other hand, all is in his head, is it not also in mine? Am I mad? Am I going to be witnessing an advanced state of my madness? Is my other self in a place I cannot avoid going? Is he where I would have been anyway without having been sucked into this mess? Is this, the whole thing, the expression of my madness? Does one see one's mind going mad from the inside? All this is too scary to even think about. I am going to stop right now.

Chapter Thirty–Two
December 15th 2001

I stayed in the cottage yesterday in order to find out about the weird room, but I have not. I still do not know whether the animal trial happened or not, so I should stay. I could go now but then I will never know. How can I, though, be more successful than yesterday? There is only one way; I have to go into the weird room with him. I think I have to do it; it is the only way. I still have a few days until the weather gets bad, and I still have the chance to leave tomorrow if I cannot handle it. I know it's crazy, but I may find a way out of all this. I have to try, at least once more.

I have been thinking about the book, of course, especially the last two words in it: "appeal denied". That is not what you say in a trial after sentencing, is it? I doubt that I just got the technicality of it wrong because in that case I would not have noticed the error now. I must have written it on purpose.

What is it, a trial or a petition for appeal? You ask for an appeal once you have been judged. Was there some sort of ellipsis between the sentence and the last two words to imply that there was some plea for appeal by somebody—the 'advocate', I suppose—which was subsequently denied? There are no lawyers in the book, and if there was an ellipsis I would have written it a bit clearer, I think. Maybe I intended to write it better, but I did not make the last correction of the text. Maybe the file I read was not the last version of the book, anyway. Perhaps it was not even the finished book. I have been assuming that the book ends by him going to Hell, but I may be wrong. The words 'The End' are not written, are they?

This is perfectly possible, because the temporary file I recovered could have been just one of the files saved while writing the book. In fact I save the documents I work on all the time when I am writing, just in case I get one of those blue screens and I lose the lot—I just saved the document at the end of last paragraph, for example. Every time I click the 'save' icon, one of those files is generated—and, if everything works well, it is deleted when I close the program. It must have been just a coincidence that the file I recovered ended in a place in the story that could have been the end of the book.

If this is the case, what else will happen? Does he go to Hell and continue writing from it? Maybe he is already in Hell, and he is just trying to get out of it. Maybe the trial is an appeal to the original trial that had already sent him to Hell, and he was just trying to go back to this world—to stop the pain. In this case, though, there is no 'this world' to come back to. In this case, this world is in Hell, and we are already in it.

Thinking about it, you cannot imagine something that

is not capable of being. You cannot imagine something that is not based on reality. If Hell exists, and it can be imagined, it must be in this world. Where did people get the idea of Hell from in the first place? All the images associated with it, and all the meanings of all the images, must have come from realities they witnessed, if not experienced.

There is nothing more evil in the imagination of the most evil person than the reality of how humans treat animals. No Nazi concentration camp, Spanish Inquisition method, fanatic terrorist attack or any other form of known evil matches the reality of the Hell we are imposing on the animal kingdom. Maybe in the book I was trying to wash my hands of it. Maybe I was trying to avoid the responsibility of it. Maybe I asked not to be considered a human, and my petition was denied. Maybe that was what I was trying to write about.

If this is Hell, if this is the Hell we have created for animals—and from seeing it with our own eyes we have imagined what the Hell that is waiting for us is like—we must then be the demons that run it. Is this what is happening? Is this who we are, demons in a Hell were innocent souls in the form of animals are tortured? Are we, human beings, the race that Evil has chosen to operate in this world?

Maybe this is what I was trying to say in the book. If the trial is not my metaphor to explain this, though, is it really happening? What if Hell is not an allegory but a reality? What if all this has nothing to do with guilt and inner ghosts, but with real cosmic powers instead? I have to find out. I have to find out about this craziness. I will go in with him tonight; it is the only way.

Chapter Thirty–Three
December 16th 2001

I am in a B&B in Inverness, going back home. I had to go, sorry, it was too much.

It took me ages to get to a train; I had to walk for miles and eventually somebody gave me a lift to the nearest town with a bus service. It is Sunday and I had to wait for quite some time to get to Kyle. I got the last train to Inverness and I had to stay here and I am going home tomorrow on the first train. Sorry, I had to do it; I had to go.

Well, I should at least write what happened—I owe it to him, I suppose.

I went to the room after dark, earlier than the time I thought he would go—I just wanted to get accustomed to the room and its weirdness. I did not sit on the orange armchair—I left that to him; instead, I sat on the long sofa. I relaxed a bit after some time, and I even got the nerve to pick up some of the books and read—I saw the red photo album and it had everything the book said.

I was browsing the album when I felt a presence in the

room. Very slowly I put the album down and I looked up. There, in the corner of the room, with a hand still on the light switch, he (me) was standing slightly trembling. I could not believe it; it was happening. I was looking at myself, at another self.

He looked around, swallowing a big gulp of saliva, and slowly made his way towards the orange armchair. He did look like me in many respects; he had glasses, very short hair and that lazy eye too. I could not believe it; this was my alter ego.

I do not know which one of us looked more nervous. He did not appear to see me — he looked a couple of times towards my face, but then quickly looked somewhere else. Now we were going to face the truth about all this. Would animals suddenly appear in the room proving that the trial was real, or would they not, proving that he just made the whole thing up from his own head?

He looked straight into my eyes. I inhaled very fast and stopped breathing for a few seconds. He kept looking at my eyes, as if he could see me now, and then he smiled.

I returned a nervous smile and I said, 'hello.'

He, with a noticeable delay, said 'hello.'

'Can you see me?' I continued.

He kept smiling with no reply. If he could see me, he obviously could not hear me. After that his eyes seemed to get lost, as if he was getting immersed in a thought or a memory — he stayed like this for a while, almost as if in some sort of trance.

I remembered the book, and then I realised what was going on. He had indeed seen me, but as he had seen me before, when I was a dog, a sheep, and perhaps a hare.

Now I was somebody else; now I was Nuska.

It was happening. I could not see the animals but he could. He could see them all, and he could see the animal I was being. I had sat on Nuska's soul; I had borrowed it; I was somehow on her or in her. It was happening; the trial was happening!

I could see the tears in his eyes, but he could not see mine. I stood up and I tried to wake him. I could touch him and I could move him, and eventually he came out of the trance, looked at me, put his hand on top of my head, and with almost no voice said, 'Hello Nuska, how are you? Where have you been?'

I could not stop weeping, but forcing myself to smile I said, 'I am fine...I am well.'

He then looked up and shouted, 'I was a child, for goodness sake! I was a child, and I loved her even after death!'

'I know...I know', I said holding him.

We both stood up holding each other and left the room. He opened the outside door, and I ran towards the trees, pretending that I was very happy. When the door closed I landed on my knees weeping, crying for my soul. That was too much; that was definitely too much.

It was extremely cold outside, so before I froze to death I came back into the house, went to the room, and I sat in a corner with all the blankets I could find. When the sun rose I took all my stuff and I left the cottage.

As I was leaving I had a last glance at the house and I saw him again. He was sitting in the kitchen frantically tapping away on his laptop. Tapping away the book that made me find him.

I left him there, sinking; gradually sinking in the mud of his own guilt. I left him there, alone, to his fate.

.

Chapter Thirty–Four
December 17th 2001

I am on a train back to Brighton and I am hoping that it will be the end of this story. I do not want to talk about it anymore, not even to think about it. I should delete the file and continue my life as always, if I can.

Delete the file, is this what happened? Is this what happened with my memory and the book? I am the one that deletes the whole thing, not him? Does this mean that from now on I will be the only one that continues with the story? Does this mean that he never comes back from the Isle of Skye, that his life ends there, that he goes to Hell from there?

This is the punishment we both deserve. I remember what he wrote when he was going to be sentenced: "Blinded by the delusion that I loved them, that I was helping them, I exploited them, I used them, I lured them into my perversions". My perversions, the perversions of humankind made mine because deep down I was aware of what I was doing. I suppose it is my awareness that makes me the worst sinner of all. When you do something wrong, it is reprovable; when you know that what you do is wrong, it is condemnable; but when you know that what you do is wrong and you disguise it as right, then, that is damnable.

If I had been a butcher, a poacher, a logging company director or a vivisectionist I would not deserve that punishment, because I would not have lived my life with the false pretences that I was dedicating it to animals. I would probably not feel guilty about anything, and that lack of guilt would not come from my evilness, but from my ignorance. My awareness makes my guilt, my guilt makes my justification, and my justification makes the flag I wave to define my cause.

I am a demon, like all humans, in a Hell where innocent animals suffer; but I am a demon that knows that he is a demon, and disguises himself as an angel. It is my deception that prompted my trial, not my faults; but I have been charged with them and no defence is possible. I said it in the book, and I have to say it now; I am guilty, I am guilty as Hell.

There is no escape from my guilt, and there is no escape from my punishment. I cannot forget; I cannot force my brain to forget. Someone said that the art of living is to master memory, to remember the right things to remember, and to forget the right things to forget. I cannot forget the right things; they always come back to haunt me. There is no escape for him – already digging his way to condemnation – and there is no escape for me either, because I am already aware of the trial. The jury will hunt me down, and sooner or later I will need to face them. I am more aware than he is, so I deserve my

Hell more than he does his.

It is so simple, and yet I refused to see it again and again. So many excuses, so many justifications; all rubbish! It is so simple; I forced myself to ignore it; nobody else did, just myself. Blaming society, blaming the world, accepting the unacceptable. It is so bloody simple!

It is all about us; about who we are, about who they are. It is about us, people. We are all people, they are all people; that is what it is. I have always known it; they are people, as we are. I have always known it, but I ignored that knowledge. Animals are people; in one way or another they are people; on one level or another they are people, and they should be treated as people. There are no excuses; there are no exceptions; they all are; they are all people...

But it does not matter anymore, because now it is too late. It is too late for him and it is too late for me. It is just too late for us, for both of us, for everybody.

***

For everybody?

For us?

For whom?

Is that it? Is the world composed of him and me? Does the universe revolve around me, the most arrogant creature ever to exist? They are people, yes, and therefore they are still out there, in this world. How can it be too late for them too? Many are still alive; many have not been born yet. They are still being chased; they are still being ignored.

I was doing it again; I was bloody doing it again! I was

ignoring them, ignoring the ones that are still out there, that are still to come. I cannot change the past but I can change the future. I cannot prevent what has been done but I can stop future wrongdoing.

What I am doing? I am here running and letting him go down; letting us go down; letting all of us go down. How can I allow that to happen? How can I accept the sentence? Are there not reasons for not accepting the sentence? Thousands of reasons; millions of reasons; all the animals that will be treated as they should not be treated. I accept the charges, but not the sentence, because if I do I would be committing a bigger sin. I would be leaving the present and future animals at the hands of demons that think they have no other choice than to torture them.

If this is the Hell in which I committed my crimes, this has to be the Hell where I will pay for them, not my private tortured Hell where my guilt completely wastes me. I accept the memories, I accept the responsibilities, and I accept the charges but I will not accept the guilt, because if I was guilty of doing wrong then I will not be guilty now of continuing to do it. How could I not see it before? It is not the past that matters but it is the present and the future. The trial does not finish with what I did in the past, the trial goes on and on until all my moral decisions have been made.

The guilt, the guilt is what stops you; the guilt is what sends you to your Hell. He did wrong and he could have done better, but he could have done even better in the future if he had not gone into Hell with his guilt. He has not been sentenced, he gave up the trial, he gave up fighting and he walked into Hell by himself!

....

Hold on, he has not done it in yet. What day is it...?
There is still time, I'm going back!

Chapter Thirty–Five
December 18th 2001

Things are going much slower than planned. Yesterday I realised that I could not catch a train back to Inverness from London. The train was delayed and was going to arrive at half past four or so at Kings Cross—the next train to Edinburgh would not get there before nine in the evening, and then I would have missed the last train to Inverness. I decided to continue to Brighton, refresh myself at home, pick up anything I would need—now I know how the weather is going to be—and take the first train to Scotland in the morning.

Today's train from Brighton was delayed—what a surprise—so I missed my connection again and I had to take the nine o'clock train to Inverness, which arrived at about six in the afternoon. Then there was a problem with the train to Kyle because of some engineering work. If I had to take the train to somewhere along the way, then take a bus to Kyle, then get to the island, and then to the cottage, all in that evening, it would have to be more than a miracle. So, I had to spend the night in

Inverness—again—where I am now writing this. The only lucky event has been that the B&B I have been using happens to be vacant every time I need it—they think I am crazy, by the way.

I hope it is not too late; I should have time before the whole process is irreversible. The problem is that although I know I have to go back and fight this thing I do not know how. I just hope that once I am there I will be inspired and I will find a way out. I have to use everything I have, in particular my brain. I have to keep thinking, and I have to keep writing because this helps me think.

There is something that I still do not get, though; my laptop. Yes, I did knock my head, and this, bizarre at it seems, might have had an effect on the way I perceive this reality. It is crazy, but not totally unbelievable, because there is nothing we see, feel or imagine that we do by bypassing our brain. Shake your brain and anything could happen. This is acceptable, but what about the laptop? It did not get knocked out, did it? Hold on, yes it did; some time before my accident the laptop did have its own accident.

It was about January or so when I was working in the office on another of my time sheets. This means that my table was totally full of stuff; the TV set connected to the video camera, this connected to the laptop, this connected to the mains, and the office computer on—all among an immense pile of paperwork. For some reason I cannot recall I stood very quickly and my foot got caught in the mains' cable that feeds the laptop. The result was catastrophic; the laptop fell flat on the floor spreading lots of pieces all over the place.

After some minor cursing—well, not that minor—I tried to put all the pieces together. It turned out to be better than I thought, since the pieces were mostly panels that could be clicked back in. The problem was the screen because it had irreparable damage; half of it had 'died' and a distinct horizontal line indicated that the glass had been cracked. The laptop was taken away for a few days—which I found very inconvenient—but came back with a brand new screen.

I have to say that the laptop has not been the same since. Every now and then some things do not work; I have problems with the infrared port, some software behaves strangely, and I get those nasty blue screens on more occasions than I used to. I was particularly fond of my laptop. I bought it when I left the Sanctuary and I planned to become freelance—I am still paying for it—and I have always been amazed by what it can do.

Now, it may seem that both laptop and I have gone through the same time shifting because we both had an accident in the office. I wonder whether or not it has anything to do with the office. Many people at work think that it is a weird place. Some don't even like to stay on their own in it—they are always sure not to be the last to go home. They say they hear mysterious sounds and all that stuff. I am naturally sceptic of this sort of thing but it is obvious that my scepticism needs some reviewing.

If I survive all this maybe I will be in a position to develop some theories that can explain some of the various paranormal phenomena that most people appear to—or believe to—have experienced at some point in their lives. Maybe parallel universes, resonating beings and temporal displacement can explain all the ghost, déjà vu experiences, premonition, telepathy, UFO and fairy phenomena, who knows? Perhaps the world will still make sense after this.

I am not sure what I am going to do when I get back in the cottage. Probably the best thing would be to go straight to the weird room and join the session. I will improvise from that point onwards. He must be with the woollies now—maybe he has finished already. Although it would be nice to see again some of the animal people I met in my life, I do not envy him at all. He is paying a huge price for it.

Chapter Thirty–Six
December 19th 2001

I am back in the cottage now. I cannot believe how long it took me to get back here — almost three days! Everything that could go wrong went wrong. The trains were booked up, delayed, industrial action, there was no train service to Kyle due to repairs, I could not find a car to take me to the cottage; it has been a nightmare.

It is late afternoon now and I am too late for today's session. I cannot see him anywhere; he must be in the other weird room, with V5. I went in mine, stayed for a while, but I could not see anything. I suppose I have to be, literally, in the right place at the right time.

It is very cloudy today; another day and I might not have made it. Firstly, because of the weather — the storm is coming and that could cut me off — and secondly because tomorrow is the last day he is going to be with any friendly animal; therefore, I have to reach him tomorrow or it could be too late. I have to do it through Nit, I have to remember where she was sitting; I have to remember!

Coming back to the whole mystery it does seem that I have managed to find a relatively acceptable explanation, after all. Well, I know that I needed some paranormal phenomena to explain the entire thing, but somehow it does make more sense with them than without them — not that I am going to abandon my natural scepticism from now on.

Let's recap. Everything started with me having the idea of writing a book well back at the beginning of this year — probably earlier than that. The next event is the laptop accident in the office, about January or so. Assuming that the office is the focus of what we could call a temporal disturbance — borrowing Star Trek terminology — because the laptop was processing information at the time of the accident, some information from the same laptop on the same desk but a few months ahead was then transferred to the laptop in February 2001. That information was a temporary file that had been saved on the 28/12/01, but as one of those computer things had not been deleted when the word processing program was closed.

By coincidence, the file corresponded to a document that ended in such a way that seemed complete — rather than a working document — and appeared to be a whole book. Due to the fact that the file/book was a temporary file — which are not normally displayed on the screen when you are looking for files — it remained hidden in the computer and I continued working unaware of its existence.

The next event is my head accident in the same office in August 2001. Because it happened in the same office, and my brain was also processing information trying to remember a zoo I had forgotten, the result was that, through the temporal disturbance, information from the future was transferred to my memory while I was unconscious. That information corresponded to my memories of writing a book on the Isle of Skye in early December of the same year. Because those memories—transferred into my brain when I was unconscious—conflicted with my normal memories my brain consequently 'labelled' them as a 'dream', and they were blocked away due to their association with a traumatic event—falling, pain, etc. When I awoke the blocking prevented me from remembering the memories (now a dream), although I had the feeling that they were important—my sub–conscious, which had access to the dream, recognised in them the book I wanted to write, and that, plus the drama of reviewing old traumas, made the forgotten information be labelled as 'important'. The result was that I continued my life as normal.

This takes us to the time I went to the Italian restaurant and the cinema—September 23rd—when I seemed to get inspired and figured out the plot of the book. In fact, what probably happened is that, for one reason or another—maybe something to do with the film—the dream/memory that was in my sub–conscious 'leaked' a bit of information into the conscious generating my inspiration (making me write what I thought was the first page of the book at that time).

A few weeks later (October 19th), when the trauma of the head accident seemed to be forgotten, and probably due to the fact that the 'leaked' information did not damage my mental ego—because everything was still a dream—the brain 'decided' to pass the memory from the sub–conscious to the conscious. The result was that I remembered the dream while microwaving some fish fingers (which played no role in the process whatsoever). I took the whole thing as a curious event, but since the label 'important' was still stuck on the memory I seriously considered the possibility of going to the Isle of Skye to follow my dream.

On November 7th a computer virus, by coincidence, drew my attention to the hidden file, and I discovered the book. Up until then everything had been fine because all was about dreams. The file, though, and the fact that it was the book I wanted to write which described the events of my dream—plus that it had a saving date of December 28th and explained very personal information that only I could have written—transformed the whole thing into a paranormal mystery.

All that happened in my universe (let's call it 'A'). There is another universe that is in fact one of the possible parallel universes (whose existence is not refuted by modern theories of quantum physics) where everything was exactly as this one up to the point where one of the previous events described did not happen. That event was the discovering of the computer file. Following quantum physics, all possible events can actually occur, and therefore, in one universe the computer virus made me find the file, and in another I do not find it.

This second universe (lets call it 'B') is the one in which I go to the Isle of Skye on December 10th unaware of the computer file (and therefore of any temporal jumping) and I begin writing the book there (not knowing that what seems like inspiration is in fact a memory). So, both versions of myself have had the knock on the head and the introduction of a future memory, but I have found out about it, and he has not.

The version of myself in universe B kept writing the book, having strange experiences and getting into so much trouble that the last I know about him is that he seems to be lost in Hell (whatever Hell is). The other version of myself (from universe 'A', the one I am writing from), following the book, managed to arrive at the Isle of Skye cottage at the same time as the other version. Due to the fact that I had a piece of information most people do not normally have (a detailed account of a future event) I discovered that parallel universes are not totally parallel; instead, there are points of connection where beings of one universe can detect beings of another, although with a slight change of shape (or species).

This extraordinary fact allowed me to witness the other version of myself getting into the process that will make him end in Hell, and after a cowardly escape and rethinking I came back in the hope that I will be able to prevent that happening (if it is possible people from parallel universes influence each other).

It makes sense, doesn't it? Apart from the fact that I had to bend most laws of Physics to arrive at this surprisingly acceptable explanation. I forgot the alternative; I am loosing my mind (and so is he).

Why have I come back? Is it out of pity, compassion or solidarity? Is it because of guilt too? Is it because of some sort of survival instinct that expands from me to my equals? It could well be, but it could also be because of defiance. A closed door is something to be opened; a lost cause is something to fight for; destiny is something to be avoided. I do not know, maybe I have lots of Mediterranean voices that call for a drama; for something to be done. The point is that I am here, and I am here to act.

Chapter Thirty–Seven
December 20th 2001

I could not reach him this afternoon; I could not; I tried, but I lost him. I did not remember where Nit was sitting in my dream, and the book did not give enough details, so I had to improvise. I thought first that I would stand and see where he was looking, but then I realised that if I was not already in resonance with one of the animals then I probably wouldn't see him coming in. I had to get in Nit from the start, or at least in one of the other animals — I was not sure whether I could change places once I was in an animal, but I thought that I probably could not.

The most likely place for Nit to sit was on the floor, probably by the fireplace. That was a wild guess, but also suited the fact that he would see her just after opening the door — as you can infer from the book. I sat there waiting. For a moment I wished I was able to see the animals myself, or at least to see Nit. If I could have her at my side, with me, rather than through me, we could fight this thing together. She would know what to do; she must have faced something similar before. I used to look at Nit when she was dreaming. I knew she was dreaming because her eyes were moving and her breathing was irregular—sometimes she even produced soundless barks. I used to wonder whether she was dreaming about wolves, her ancestors, the bearers of her true self; if they were telling her what to do, how to deal with the pack, when is the right night to howl, and all that. I wished she were there with me to tell me.

Eventually the door opened. He did not look good; his beard had grown and he looked pale and scruffy. I knew he had gone through a rough time so far, but that was nothing compared to what was waiting for him in a few days' time. His face resembled mine more than before—I suppose I was not looking very good either. Before sitting on the orange armchair he stared in my direction which made me think I got the right spot; he must have seen Nit in me. He sat smiling at me and got into the daydreaming state.

I then stood up trying to awake him, to communicate with him, but when I touched his arm he suddenly disappeared. I must have fallen out of resonance with Nit's soul; I must have stood up too fast, and I fell out of her. I sat again in the same spot, moving a bit to the right and to the left, but all in vain. Nobody else would appear in the room for that evening. I had blown it; I had been too impatient, and I had totally blown it.

How can I help him? What can I do from this universe? Can I stop it without getting to him? Can I stop Hell? Can I face Evil and defeat it? I am just a human, how can I? How can a single person confront one of the major forces of the world we live in, of the reality we are all made of?

If somebody is going to defeat Evil, is this not the role of a demon? Maybe it is not a matter of saving souls, but a matter of converting demons. If Lucifer managed to successfully revolt against God, why cannot a demon revolt against Lucifer, and win? Why cannot Hell undergo a mutiny?

All is not lost. I still have tomorrow's session. I know that tomorrow is the day when things start getting nasty, but there will be still animals in the room—millions of them, in fact. I have to try to resonate with the sheep, the sheep that guides him up the hill. I have to try to guide him out of there, to connect with him, to talk to him. If I cannot do it tomorrow I do not know when I will be able to.

How many times do we find ourselves in this situation? Never, you may think, but is it really never? How many times do we face strangers in ourselves, or ourselves in people we know? How many times do we run from ourselves? How many times do we abandon ourselves to what we call 'fate'? It is not that uncommon. OK, these scenarios do not normally take the form of a real interaction between two separated entities, as in my case, but the essence of the struggle is not that different.

There are many people in our own heads. We are plural creatures, you know? Not just the people we have met and we remember, but also the people we were before our personality limited us; the people we were before we evolved into who we are today; the people we share genes with, the people we share experiences with, the people we share the planet with. All of them are voices that sometimes sing together, and at other times they all sing their own songs. Sometimes the singing is so confusing—like loud cowbells in your head—that it makes you run from it into a place where a louder noise can block it. But there is a voice among the crowd that is always in tune; a voice that never lets itself be dragged away from the main melody, from the great song of all. Many people use different terms to describe that voice. I like to call it 'common sense'.

Chapter Thirty–Eight

December 31st 2001

I cannot take the dream out of my mind. I do not know what is happening to me. I should delete it from my memory; it is interfering too much with my work. For instance, I was recently torturing a mortal when I thought I heard its cry. I know they do cry, they cry all the time, but we demons cannot hear it. It is well below our sensitive threshold — it is just as well, otherwise it would be very annoying to listen again and again to that horrible sound.

I must have imagined it, probably influenced by my dream, but it did feel real, a real cry. It is not just that. On another occasion I had the impression that one of the mortals saw me. I know they can see us up to a point; they see our blades, fire, stones and everything we use on them — it is part of the torture to see it coming — but they should not see that behind all that there are intelligent entities that operate them. They do not know that demons exist; they might think we exist, or they might have thought we exist, but they cannot see us, and therefore they do not know about our existence. Something would be wrong if they could see us; that would mean that part of them is not in total pain yet.

Maybe I have not been doing my job properly. Maybe I have not paid enough attention lately, and I have left some of the mortals under–tortured. It must be the dream again. It is becoming an obsession. It is as if I have been infected by thoughts of time, cause, guilt...It is as if I have been possessed by a mortal soul. I wonder how I can delete my dream.

Where are demon dreams stored, anyway? Not that we have a brain we can squash — it would be fun if we could. We are not made of flesh and bone as the mortals. We have a higher nature, we are made of energy, energy contained in an ethereal cloud of pure identity. Our individuality is expressed through the awareness and transcendence of spiritual consciousness. We are blessed with the gift of eternal life. Our memory must be kept in pockets of cosmic energy, or something like that. Can I delete them? Can I push a button and delete my dream?

I cannot delete my memory because I am a demon; I do not have remorse. How can I have acquired a memory that I later do not want? By remembering the memory I want to forget, the memory comes back unchanged. Why am I bothered with this dream, anyway? I do not care if some mortals appear to see me or not. I do not care if I can hear their screams. Why should I care, anyway?

Maybe I should care because if other demons see that I am thinking all this, that I am imagining mortals noticing me and I noticing them, I could be in trouble. They could call the Boss, and that could have very bad consequences for me. I am not sure what He would do, but He could move me to another pit with fewer mortals to torture; or He could send me to posses a mortal when it's being tortured. I do not know. Do other demons have the same problems? I do not think so.

I have to go back to work...this mortal here, for instance. I know its pain does not allow it to see beyond the blade, but if you look at it, it does appear to be looking at me, does it not? It does appear to see me, as if it knows that I pull the rope. If I stare at it long enough it even seems as if it is trying to say something to me. It does not look like a normal mortal, though. To be honest, it looks more like a demon than a mortal.

Wait a moment, this is a demon, this is not a mortal, what is he doing in my pit? Why is he not moving? I know he has seen me; this is obviously my pit, but he does not seem to go anywhere. It is a funny looking demon, though. He should be torturing mortals and not looking at me like that. He does have some mortal looking features—this is why I confuse him at first. Anyway, enough wondering. Back to work.

Chapter Thirty–Nine

December 21st 2001

He did not listen to me; he did not appear to see me any more. When I was in the weird room, supposedly being the sheep in the immense hall, I tried to guide him away from the trial, but it did not work. When he left the room I went with him, and then through the main door to see whether he would follow me out — as he did in the room while I was moving about — but he went straight upstairs, to the bedroom. I went back in and I followed him.

I talked to him when he was getting into bed — with all his clothes on. I called him, I asked him to leave the cottage, I explained to him that he was in great danger, but he did not seem to hear me at all. When I touched or grabbed him I realised I was totally incapable of moving him, but he would notice my touch because he would gently push me away with the back of his hand. He did not hit me; he smoothly pushed me away with the back of his hand. I recognised the gesture; this is what I do when a mosquito tries to sting me.

I could not reach him, I could not reach him at all, but I kept talking to him again and again. Maybe in the deepest trenches of his consciousness my words could find fertile soil, so I did not give up for a while.

I told him about guilt. I told him that guilt is not a path to redemption but to condemnation. In what way does guilt prevents the event that generates it? How can something that has been done be changed through guilt? Memory teaches, not guilt. Recognising what is a mistake can only be done when one is free from the guilt of it. You cannot be guilty of an error, a misjudgement, or the result of your inexperience or stupidity. You only can be guilty of an act of bad faith; an act intrinsically conceived to achieve wrongdoing; an act intimately nourished through evil in any of its forms. Such acts cannot be corrected because they lack causality; such acts cannot be amended because you cannot learn from them. But you can learn from mistakes if you free them of guilt. Only when the guilt is gone can the mind think, find the causes, find the effects, find the consequences, and recognise the problem. Then you can act on that problem and be redeemed of your mistakes.

Guilt forces you to accept that you are incapable of doing better. Guilt is the end of the moral judgement, stopping it, preventing it finding the right thing to do. Guilt only comes when the action is all done, when the problem has lost its chances of solution. Guilt is what pushes you to the pit, what drives you into Hell, and what keeps you there for eternity. We walk into Hell by ourselves, nobody sends us there.

If you do not smile at life, life is not going to smile

back at you. Even through the horrors of your own guilt the smile is more effective than the tear. The smile does not prevent you recognising the mistakes or accepting the responsibilities. The smile does not make you forget what you have done. What the smile gives you is the courage to correct the mistake. The smile gives you hope, and hope gives you the chance to find the right thing to do. There are no optimists in Hell; they all escaped with a smile.

Tomorrow I may totally lose him. His universe must be in the process of disconnecting from mine. The darkness, the darkness that appears in the book, will stop him seeing anything else other than the contorted crevices of his cave. No animal will reach him there; not one soul can.

I do not know whether all my talking will have any effect. I just do not know enough about this world of ghosts and resonating entities. I know that one of the reasons I can see him is that we are very similar. This is why we do not normally see people that appear and disappear. The similarity between entities may make the resonance more likely, but the appearance of similar entities when they see each other may change considerably from one universe to another. The reason that I see him as a person such as me, and he sees me as an animal instead, must be the fact that I am aware of who he is, and my brain constructs an image that is more compatible with my idea of him. Since his brain is not aware of me, it does not need to make his mental image closer to my own image. This would also explain why the more I see him the more he resembles me.

All this experience is giving me a completely new perspective about how our brain works. We do not see the world out there through our senses; we see it through our brain. Yes, I am aware most people know that it is the brain that perceives what the senses get, but it is not just perception. Our brain invents the world and uses information provided by our senses to check whether the interpretation of it is consistent with the real world. We see the world inside, and then we check whether outside there is a similar world. We basically dream the world and cross–reference it with reality through our senses. There are entities out there that move around, and our brain gives them shape. That shape is who we interact with; but every now and then our senses check whether there is still somebody out there behind that shape; sometimes there is, and sometime there is not. This is fascinating.

If this is the way it works maybe his senses, when cross–referencing me to check who I am, are able to pick up that I am actively interacting with him, that I am trying to reach him. Maybe his brain will ignore it, or will incorporate the new information either as a real interaction with me whatever shape I have — I am thinking now of the occasion I saw the first *Polistes* looking at me — or somewhere in the sub conscious instead. Either way I should still try to reach him; I should try again tomorrow.

Chapter Forty
December 22nd 2001

I have not seen him any more. I went to the weird room but I could not see him. Today was the day of the desert, so there was not a soul to interact with him at all, as I suspected. I do not think I will be able to do it again. He is too deep in it now; from now on there are no more animals, friendly or not; from now on the rest of the way is too steep down.

I could still try to get him when he is out of the room, but I do not think there is going to be any animals around, or that he would pay any attention to them if that were the case. His mind is already lost.

I have failed him. I could have stopped him in time; if I only had stayed, rather than run away like a coward, I could have stopped him, I know I could. But I did not.

No, I have not failed him. I have not failed him because it is not over. There is no guilt if the problem is not finished; I said it to him, and I almost forgot it myself. If the problem remains the chances of solution are still there. I have to think. What else do I have? I have to think. Who else do I have?

I am not totally alone in this; I never was, from the start. I would not have landed into this muddle if it had not been for someone else, something else; the laptop. It has been going through the same ordeal since it fell from my desk. Can I use it to reach him? Let's reflect on it.

It is obvious that as far as the temporal distortion is concerned, it does not matter whether the entity that can retain information from the future is organic or inorganic—as long as it is capable of processing and storing information it seems possible. I know what the effects of these temporal jumps are on a biological creature such as me. I also know the implications in terms of surfing between two universes, but I do not know how a digital brain reacts to all this. If I can recognise my alter ego, can my laptop recognise its alter ego too (there are two laptops here, the one I am using right now, and the one he is using when he writes), if there is such thing?

I am not inferring that the laptop has personality and therefore ego, but it does have a particular combination of programs installed, many of my files in its memory, and has been suffering glitches here and there that could shape, in one way or another, its circuits. I presume that it is possible that my laptop is now unique and distinct from any other laptop in my world. Would that in itself constitute a level of individuality that could generate the equivalent of the soul–resonance I have been experiencing? The laptop may not have consciousness that allows it to recognise itself, or its other self, but I do. If I operate the laptop I could try to see whether I can network it to its other version and maybe I could establish a communication link between two universes.

I should use the original file, the temporary file that I discovered with the book. That file might have something slightly different in its structure that will make the processor crash. If I crash the laptop system in the same spot where the other laptop is at the very moment he is writing the famous file, when I reboot my laptop maybe it can 'resonate' with the other and I can write in both at the same time. Maybe I can write to my other self. It sounds crazy, but no crazier than the rest of the stuff that has already been going on here.

This means that firstly I have to sit where he was sitting while writing—I know the spot because I saw him writing before I left. Secondly, I have to find in my laptop the original temporary file—I know it is still there. Thirdly, I have to wait until December 28th, which is the day the temporary file was created in his laptop. Finally, I have to manage to crash the computer system while writing on the document saved in the temporary file and then quickly reboot bypassing all normal diagnostics to see whether the file is still there and has resonated with its original version. From that point onwards I will need to improvise.

How I am going to crash the computer system, though? It is not something we can do; it happens when something goes wrong, or sometimes for no apparent reason—there is always a reason, but it is not evident to the user. There is another way; a computer virus; of course, this is how I discovered the file in the first place; the file had a virus that made the laptop crash. The problem is that I cleared the virus and now it is not in the file any more. I know what I have to do; I have to remember the name of the virus, then go to the program that cleans them (which has a copy of all viruses so it can compare them with the file to clean), extract the virus and put it back to the temporary file.

Damn! I do not remember the virus name. My memory again, this cannot happen to me right now. I do not care whether I burn toast or lose umbrellas, but this is something different. I have to remember the name of that virus; I have to concentrate and remember.... I have to think; I have to smile and think.

Chapter Forty–One
January 1st 2002

Maybe you need to be a trans–cultural creature to be able to have a trans–specific approach to the world. Perhaps when life forces you to review your identity, it is then a good opportunity to look at who we really call 'we'. Could it all be a matter of pronouns, nouns, or labels?

Who are 'we' anyway? It is easy to say who 'I' am, but who are 'we'? When does the 'we' stop and become 'they'? Where is the boundary? How many entities can the pronoun 'we' hold? We call ourselves demons, and we call them animals; or mortals—mortals, animals, what is the difference? Whatever they are, they are not 'we', are they?

Take this demon over here, for example. I thought he was a mortal, but it turned out to be a demon. Although he has the appearance of any other demon, he does not behave like any demon. He does not torture animals as I do. Look at him, he does not do it. He just watches.

He does not clip the testicles of cats, break the instincts

of horses, explode the stomachs of geese, corrupt the liver of guinea pigs, pull the necks of dogs, cut the wings of ducks, burn the eyes of rabbits, chop the horns of rhinos, cut the heads of rats, choke the breath of trout, break the back of donkeys, burst the hearts of deer, steam the bodies of lobsters, stab the backs of bulls, blaze the homes of woodpeckers, pull the teeth of elephants, rip the body of foxes, bolt the brains of sheep, slash the throats of pigs, pull the wings of butterflies, vanish the life of dodos, infect the lungs of chimps, jab the sides of tuna fish, cut the hands of gorillas, oil the lungs of cormorants, smash the skulls of seals, fry the brains of monkeys, harpoon the backs of whales, break the minds of polar bears, roast the bodies of chickens, poison the eggs of sparrows, impale the bodies of beetles, strip the skins of leopards, sever the tails of rays, boil the legs of frogs, crush the heads of snakes, pulverise the bones of tigers, suffocate the gulls of goldfish, stuff the guts of turkeys, boil the shells of mussels, suck the bladders of bears, burst the chests of pheasants, poison the blood of mice, skin the furs of chinchillas and all the other things we do to animals all the time.

He does not do any of that. He just looks at the animals, and looks at me. How can he be a demon if he does not do what demons do? How can I include him when I say 'we'? On the other hand he does look like me, like a demon, and he does appear to see me; he does recognise my individuality as only a demon can do. I cannot take him out of 'we' and consider him an animal, can I?

So who are we, and who are they? What do the animals think they are? Do they use the term 'we'? Do they speculate about us, about the creatures behind the fire? Before they fall into our hands do they fear the possibility of our existence? Do they imagine us as ghosts, haunting them, spying on them, following them around, setting traps for them to fall in? What do they think about us before the pain makes them forget us?

Maybe if I try to remember my dream again, I would remember how they see us...no, I do not remember. What was that word? There was a term I cannot recall exactly; there was a word to describe something...ah yes, 'human'; the word is 'human'. What does it mean?... Probably nothing.

* * *

That other demon is still here. He has not tortured anyone yet and he is driving me crazy. What is that light in front of me? It is like a blur, quite faint; like a small cloud of fuzzy light; I have seen it before, but now it is a little bit clearer.

That thing about 'we' I was talking about; what if both demons and animals are the same kind of creatures, such as pieces in the game of existence? Then it would be appropriate to use the term 'we', wouldn't it? Not that I can imagine any situation when I would have to use it to mean that, but I could if I wanted, couldn't I? Maybe 'we' could both go through similar processes in our existence even if we remain as distinct groups. We could all have the same dreams, for example. I could dream I am a mortal, and they could dream they are demons (that light in front of my face is annoying me now).

Therefore, in the same way I dreamt I was an animal, an animal could dream that it was a human, I mean a

246

demon (that word again, I do not know why it popped out there). That animal would then remember what it is like to live for eternity, torture others, feel no remorse, and have no free will. How could that animal continue living its life as before? It is the same thing that happened to me, is it not? Since that dream I do not seem to have been back to my usual self. We could both be suffering the same confusion. Neither of us would really be back in our own world. In fact, I would have more in common with that animal than with the other humans. That animal and I could be 'we'. Who would torture whom then? If none of us would torture the other, we would both be animals; otherwise we would both be demons? (This is very confusing, and this floating light is not making it easier either).

What does BI U mean? What is all that? Normal? What is normal? Times New Roman? The 'A' with the thing underneath; and the numbers...I know this.... No, I don't. The wind, where did the wind come from? Ah, that thing here...and the arrow....

...I am a human, aren't I?.... We humans rule Hell....

STOP TYPING, STOP TYPING NOW, YOU ARE NOT MAKING ANY SENSE

Who....

DO NOT TYPE, ONLY READ

I am....

DO NOT TYPE AGAIN, DO YOUR HEAR ME?

THIS IS THE END OF YOUR TYPING. YOU CANNOT TYPE ANY MORE, UNDERSTOOD?

....

THAT'S BETTER; GOOD BOY.

NOW, FOLLOW THESE LINES OVER HERE. KEEP MOVING; THAT'S RIGHT; A LITTLE BIT MORE. OK STOP. NOW PUT YOUR HEAD IN HERE; DON'T MOVE IT NOW; IT'S GOING TO BE MUCH WORSE IF YOU MOVE IT. THAT'S BETTER; GOOD BOY.

LET'S PUT THIS IN HERE TOO; AND THAT.

YOUR ARE AN ANIMAL NOW, SO WE ARE GOING TO TAKE CARE OF YOU FROM NOW ON. SAY GOOD BYE.

Stop! Stop right now!

WHO ARE YOU?

It does not matter who I am. Stop and leave him alone!

YOU CAN'T....

Yes I can. Now I am the one typing here, and I will be deleting anything else that appears in the screen.

....

I told you that I would delete it. Now, stay away from him. Step back and do not get close to him. You, take your head out from whatever it is in now, and get rid of anything that ties you. Have you done it? You can type to reply to me.

....

Not you, him!

Yes, I am not tied up any more. Who are you?

It is difficult to explain and we have no time. Just trust me. You have to get out of wherever you are now, do you understand? Can you see any doors?

No...what I can see is many of these creatures coming towards me. What are they? What should I do now?

Umm...is there any place you can go? A corridor, a ladder, under something....

No, I am surrounded now...they are all coming...they are very close...there is no place to go.

Let me think; let me think...that's it! Growl, growl and bite; that's right, bite them! Bark, growl and bite them! Push them away with your paws, and bite them as hard as you can! Bite them all!! No matter how many come to you, keep biting, keep growling, and keep barking. Do not give up, you hear, do not give up! You fight down there, and I will howl for help. Now, now is the right night for howling!

....

Are you still there?

Yes. They have all gone. I bit them as you said. I growled and bit them. I heard a howl, and then many more howls coming from the distance, filling this place. They ran away, all of them. Who are you? Are you...Nit?

...Yes, I am

Where are you?

I am here; can't you see me?

Ah yes, I can; here you are. I have missed you! Have I done well? Have I fought well?

Yes you have, you protected the pack well. I am proud of you. Can you see the light better now? The light is your laptop, you know? Go and get it.

I've got it now, it's right here.

Can you see it well?

It is a bit blurry.

Look at it deeply; keep focusing on it.

Nit?

Yes?

Am I in Hell?

No, you are not; you are in a cottage in the Scottish Highlands. Look around, can you see it?

Yes, I can now. I can see the window, and I can see the sun. It is that time the sun likes to hide below the horizon and stay there for a while, teasing you with colours, making you stop whatever you are doing. It is the time the sun likes to smile. Yes, I can see it; I can see it smiling.

Keep looking at it and listen. Behaving ethically is not about past, it is about future. It is not about remorse, repentance or redemption; it is about how to do Good; it is about how to choose well. Your experience will teach you about causes and effects, but each individual moral decision has to be made with an open heart and an awakened mind. The right decisions are not written anywhere, you will not find them in any religion, doctrine or belief. Ethics is about thinking about what you are going to do, not thinking about what you have already done. You do have free will to choose, but free will is not about being free to choose your destiny; free will is about having the chance to freely choose the right decision. The right decision is free; it is free for everybody, from the microbe to the demon. Nothing stops us doing right, not even Evil can.

I understand it now, but I did do wrong things, I cannot deny them.

Yes, you did, and you should never forget them, but you have to do better now; you do not have excuses anymore. You have amends to make, you have problems to solve, you have battles to win; you still have time; there is still time. People are animals, and animals are people; if you always remember this you will choose right and you will do right.

What about the trial then? What about the sentence?

We did not sentence you; we did not come to judge you; we came because you asked us to come. It is you; it has always has been you.

What about the others, what about the world?

The others can choose too. The right decisions are free for them too. It is easier than it seems. It may take just a couple of seconds. If everybody stopped at the same time whatever they are doing, for just a couple of seconds, to look at who is at the end of their guns, on their plates, under their knives, in the enclosure they are watching, on the side of the road they are passing, in the tank they are feeding, in the fire they are burning, under their feet, on their hands, in front of their eyes and then think, for just those two seconds, of what they are doing, of what they were going to do, and of what they really want to do, that would be enough. That would be as long as it would take for the common sense music to reach their minds, and when that happens Evil itself will choose another place to go.... We have to go now, keep focusing in the cottage, and keep smiling to the sun.

Nit?

Yes?

Before you go....

It's all right, don't worry, it's all right

* * *

I found myself sitting in the kitchen, in front of the laptop. The sun had just come out, and the purple planet was purpler than ever. Most of the clouds had gone — only a few lazy ones wandered about as if they had nothing to do with the others. The island grass seemed to have enjoyed the rain, and I am sure the cattle would appreciate that.

The table was full of books, pieces of paper, dictionaries, floppies, pens, markers and tea stains. The kitchen sink was about to be sick, but nothing that could not be sorted out with a little bit of cleaning. The laptop hurricane had already been imprinted in my ear, so even through it I could still hear the silence — I never managed to get rid of the smell of burnt rice, though. One apple and two oranges left. 'Not bad at all', I thought, 'not bad at all.'

I guess this is it. I have done it. I have written a book. I have delivered the baby, and now it is out there, in the world — it is a little weak though, and like all babies still needs lots of care.

I knew I could do it; I knew I could write it — you already knew that bit, but I did not.

I have learnt; I have learnt about many things on this journey.

I'll be packing this afternoon and I will leave the cottage in the morning. By tomorrow evening I should have left the purple planet.

I have lots to do in the other planet. I am sure that there are plenty of cases waiting for me in the office — there are plenty of animals out there that need help, you know? There are also many things to change, many situations to improve and many right decisions to make.

Ah, and I have to go to the doctors and check my head as well.

Well, I'll be going now.

I'd better tidy the cottage up because I have invited the sun for dinner this evening.

It was nice to write to you.

ISBN 1412086361-1

9 781412 086363